# The 13<sup>th</sup> Victim

Reneé Porter

Roet Press

A Roet Press Publication

ISBN: 0615483488
ISBN-13: 978-0615483481 (Roet Press)

*For Rob, with love*

# ACKNOWLEDGEMENTS

Were it not for the strong women in my life, this book might never have been written. Much thanks to my cover artist, Elizabeth Mott, whose unflinching bravery, intelligence, and discipline inspire me each day; and, to those women who believed in me when I could scarce believe in anything. Thanks to them: Pamela Sahdev, who never stopped telling me to write; Tami Varney, who gave me her love and support; and finally to my mother, Peggy, and my sister, Jane, who were the first to listen.

To John Teel, my first true editor, and Julia Thomas, my dear friends who were there in the very beginning.

And finally to Rob, my life and my love, who supported me in every way possible, including listening every night to the incredible neuroses with which we writers torture ourselves.

# CHAPTER 1

Technically, she was not dead. Of course, she was not dead. Otherwise, she would not be reading on the internet that she was. She looked up from the laptop and out the bay window at the pasture and the gray sleet that deadened the mountains and the distant tree line, the ice crusting over the already graying snow that neither melted nor grew with the cold February day.

She thought of the horses that she would need to go visit later in the afternoon and dreaded the short trudge through the snow and mud and ice between the house and the barn. Even the red and white barn painted just two years ago faded into the muted light of the Sunday afternoon.

Looking back at the laptop screen, Pearl Marie Taliaferro Montgomery, known since she was nine as "Pea", curled her legs beneath her on the oversized red suede sofa and began to read again about her disappearance and probable death. The short internet blurb led to a longer article posted in yesterday's *Staunton Dispatch*. The newspaper article related the story of Pearl Marie Montgomery, 20, of Staunton, Virginia, who had disappeared June 1, 1998, from an area along Route 11, just outside of Staunton. The article went on to mention that Pearl Marie Montgomery had previously been arrested twice for possession of narcotics. The newspaper included information on Pearl's family, acquaintances, and the usual ineffective quote from law enforcement that had probably stopped their search for Pearl the month she disappeared. There was also a photograph of Pearl that was obviously a mug shot from one of her previous arrests, as well as a picture of a middle-aged black man, wearing a cracked leather coat and a Virginia Tech Hokies baseball cap, his face worn and as wrinkled as his coat. He was surrounded by what appeared to be Pearl's other family members.

The photograph of Pearl's family disturbed Pea the most. Their distress, their not knowing, their worry and pain were evident even with the passage of the 12 years since Pearl had disappeared. The man in the picture held a sheet of paper from which he appeared to be reading. Pea could imagine a slight tremor in his hand as he read from the paper, asking for any help, any information, just anything that would relieve his worry.

The photograph of Pearl was a strong contrast to the other photo. Pearl glared from the laptop screen, her face angrily defiant, but her eyes appearing sad and a bit confused. She looked older than the 20 years she actually was when the mug shot was taken. In the photograph, her brown skin looked dull, her short brown hair matted and flat. Pea believed that before the drugs and what ever she had stumbled upon that Pearl had probably been quite pretty. Even with the dull, prematurely aged skin, an underlying bone structure told of a Pearl that might have been, a happier child and teenager who had maybe once dreamed about dolls and dates instead of drugs.

Unknowingly, Pea sighed, the only sound in the house other than the quiet snores from her two Harlequin great danes sleeping beneath her, their huge bodies sprawled across the antique, wide, golden oak floorboards like black and white blankets, the rise and fall of their great barrel chests moving like small waves against the shore of the oak.

How odd, Pea thought. A woman, the same age as she, with her name, had disappeared on her birthday 12 years ago and less than two hours away from where she sat now. Where was Pea 12 years ago? She knew without hesitation. Her 20th birthday. She had spent it here with her teen age sister, Mary Alicia Taliaferro, whom she called Ree, and her parents.

It had been a spectacular June day as most Greenbrier County June days were. Warm, but not hot, with the slight promise of a thunderstorm later that night. She was happy that day in a way that now no longer seemed even a remote possibility. Not because it was her birthday, but because she was with those she loved in the place she loved the most of anywhere she had ever been.

Pea was not a traveler. A student at William and Mary, she loved the school and the campus, but it was not home. No place was home but the family farm with its 600 acres and adjacent Anthony Creek Stables. Home to her was on the back of a horse, riding through the pastures around the farm. She preferred the quiet of West Virginia's Greenbrier Valley, the comfortable knowledge that things there would be as they had been for the over 200 years her family had lived there. Mary often teased her about it and told her she was stuck in *Green Acres* land. Mary was beginning her senior year of high school with a dream of law school, politics and world travel. I can always visit, Mary would say, but for Pea, visits were for everywhere but here.

Pea's fiancée, Manley, was back at school, packing for a summer trip home. Pea felt lucky that Manley seemed just as happy to settle with her at the family home. Although a native of La Terre, Louisiana, he told Pea that she was what he wanted and where ever she was would be his home. They had met at a Greek party his fraternity was having with her sorority. He was a Pike, a Pi Kappa Alpha, and she was a Tri-Sigma. He was someone she had known for a year or so and their eventual joining had seemed inevitable. He was handsomely dark, tan, and athletically thin with conversational skills that complemented Pea's shyness. Alone, they were able to find similar interests and dreams. At 20, she had thought that sharing each other and love were enough.

Thinking back on that June day, she wondered what the other Pearl Marie had been doing. Had she been happy? Sad? Looking for release in a crack pipe? Had either of them really had a chance after that day, she asked herself.

She closed the laptop before the tears could come. All she ever wanted was a quiet life here with a family, a man who loved her, children to raise, a small garden to tend. Nothing big or important. Not to be famous or rich. Just a wife and mother who taught horseback riding to children, to run the family farm, with a life full of children and animals and Manley. Manley.

He was gone. Her parents gone. Her sister gone. Even most of the horses now gone. Just her, an empty house with two snoring dogs and an internet newspaper story that told her that she, too, was gone.

Well, hadn't she known that already? She had disappeared with the other Pearl Marie that same day and hadn't even known until now that she was gone.

Her disappearance took 12 years and began June 1, 1998 as well. That night her parents had driven to The Greenbrier Resort for dinner with friends after her afternoon cake and presents. Their maroon Volvo had swerved on the wet road from the thunderstorm that had finally presented itself in its full glory, landing in the late spring high waters of the Greenbrier River. The car was found a few miles downstream near Ronceverte the next morning. Pea and Mary had woken to sharp knocking on the heavy tiger stripe maple front door of their home. The sheriff's deputy held his hat in his hands and couldn't meet their eyes as he related the details of their parents' deaths. He looked out to the road to his squad car as if to escape their grief. Death notifications required something that he lacked. Not tact or sympathy, but just the awful bravery it took officers to face mortality in the tears of others.

Manley rushed from school to her side, guided them through everything, leading them to the Honaker Funeral Home and selecting coffins, to florists, and churches and their minister and music and obituaries. On one side he held Pea up throughout the services while Mary stood to her other side. Her life had changed then. Lawyers, wills, probate, an entire summer filled with death. She remembered the strangest things from that summer. Not ceremonies nor meetings or even her decision to leave school and take on the farm. Instead, if she thought about it now, 12 years later, the things she remembered most was sitting at the family's baby grand playing Billy Joel's *Lullabye* every day, riding the trail along Anthony Creek and watching the leaves floating away toward the Greenbrier, thinking that the leaves would follow the Greenbrier to the New River to the Mississippi and then eventually to the Gulf of Mexico. The leaves and the lullabye.

While Manley prepared to return to Louisiana for a briefer than planned visit, she eventually woke from her grief that summer and began the daily responsibilities of running the farm. Her parents had divided the estate equally between their daughters, but Mary quickly stepped up and told Pea that she couldn't, wouldn't, take on the farm. It's always been yours, Green Acres, she said. And truly there was enough money for both of them for a lifetime, even one without the farm, but even at 17, Mary understood that Pea could not survive the loss of their parents and the farm so she "gave" it to Pea with only the verbal promise to come home as often as possible so Pea wouldn't be alone.

Manley gave the same promise, though it was only later that Pea realized he had wanted her to sell everything and leave the Greenbrier Valley forever. Later that summer he had taken her to his home in La Terre to meet his "mama" and unknown to her at the time, to try to convince her to abandon the idea of running the farm.

His mother, Laura, could not have been more gracious or sympathetic to her loss or more encouraging of the marriage next spring of Manley and Pea.

Laura, however, had insisted on calling Pea "Pearl" and had spent long hours talking about her own family, her dead husband and dead daddy. She questioned Pea about her plans, about her sister's entailment of the family property, would she really want to run the farm with children? Was West Virginia really sophisticated enough for her and Manley to make the life they wanted for their children? Louisiana, after all, had so much culture to offer beyond a horse farm and a five star hotel, she would say.

Pea had smiled and ignored Laura when Laura began her daily campaign to bring them to La Terre. Pea loved Manley, but she knew that she could not leave her family home. It was where she was born. It was where she probably would die and be buried in the family plot. Maybe she wasn't sophisticated, but she was smart enough to see Laura's plans. When she complained to Manley, he just shrugged it off and said "That's just mama. Don't worry about it. We'll do fine."

So she believed him. She believed him for ten years, through the birth of their daughter, Alicia Marie, through her daily running of the farm, through her garden club meetings and church duties, through his long hours working at the hotel and her horseback camps, through two miscarriages, and finally through the death of their daughter, Alicia, at the age of six.

Then she discovered that her ideal life was a lie. The fights began shortly after the Lexington Horse Show where little Alicia rode for the first time in competition. Something so simple. Just once around the track on her gentle Palomino, wearing her red habit proudly, her head held high until a noise spooked the horse and he reared up, throwing Alicia back onto the hard packed Virginia clay, her neck breaking like a stick of kindling.

They had airlifted her small body to the University of Virginia hospital, but it had been too late the moment the horse reared up. The doctors asked about organ transplants and neither parent could respond. Mary, who had driven from Lexington to Charlottesville faster than anyone could have conceived, took them together and helped them agree to the transplant and then drove them the three hour trip home without their baby.

Alicia was buried next to her grandparents. Pea visited her daily. Manley pretended the plot did not exist.

Manley began to stay away and Pea began to hear the whispers to which she had previously, intentionally, deafened herself. When she discovered that he had had numerous affairs during their ten year marriage, including an off-again, on-again affair with a girl he had been engaged to at William and Mary before he met Pea, she filed for divorce. She told him she would not charge him with adultery if he walked away quietly. He yelled, threatened her with legal action, and finally demanded a substantial settlement for his "help" with the farm. In the end, she gave him $150,000 and told him to go back to Louisiana and never remind her that they had ever been married.

Now, almost two years later, she had almost shut the farm down. Only three of her horses were left and the family land was rented out to local cattle farmers for grazing. Pea closed the stables to the public, stopped attending her club meetings and church and became reclusive to the point that her only time away from the farm was a weekly evening trip to Lewisburg to Kroger's or a trip to Charleston, West Virginia every few months to have her hair trimmed. Anything to avoid other people who knew her failure as a mother and wife and daughter. Anything to avoid a reminder of the life that she had lost. She could not let them see her tears and so even her existence faded away into the past gossip of garden club meetings and a vague memory of the Taliaferro family.

She and Mary Alicia were the last Taliaferros in Greenbrier County. Mary Alicia was gone and now, according to the *Staunton Dispatch*, so was she. She thought about that for a few moments, even touching her cheek to see if she was really there and for the first time in what seemed like two years she laughed out loud. She placed the laptop on the glass table beside the sofa and rustled the dogs from their sleep to go check the horses.

I'm not dead, she said out loud. I'm not dead. But she wondered if the other Pearl Marie had said those words. It wasn't much comfort and as Pea began to feed the horses, she also began for the first time in 12 years to think about anything other than what she had come to call "her own useless life."

No, I'm not dead. I'm not. I'm not. She was whispering those words over and over to herself quietly, as she softly stroked the forelock of the palomino.

# CHAPTER 2

*June 1998*

Pearlie Montgomery was sweating profusely. She hadn't bathed in a few days and her dark skin reeked of cigarettes, acetone, and crack smoke. Her hair was matted with sweat and dirt and smelled almost as bad as her body did. It was humid and Staunton Boulevard felt like it was a hundred degrees in the late afternoon sun.

She had walked from her Momma's apartment downtown, past the Veterans' Cemetery and down the three miles to Route 11, the gray dust from the roadside coating her brown feet with an ashy film over the dirt from the last week. One red toenail hung over the left pink flip-flop as she walked.

Fucking LeeAnn.

"Don't give her money, Momma. She'll just end up at Downey's sucking crack."

Her own sister didn't give a shit about her. Well, fuck LeeAnn. Fuck her whole family, she thought. She didn't need their help. She'd get over to Downey's on her own and maybe if she gave him a little suck, then he'd give her a little suck on the pipe. She giggled as she stumbled along the road and looked down at the purple-blue Chicory growing next to her feet.

She sobered up for a moment and remembered Granny Mabel telling her about making Chicory coffee during the depression. Granny Mabel had taught her a lot of stuff – how to make good, sweet cornbread in her old iron skillet, to always wear a hat to Sunday School, and not to think that she wouldn't get switched for talking back. Granny Mabel would have switched her from one side of Staunton to the other if she knew what Pearlie was going to do.

She looked up to the intersection of Staunton Boulevard and Route 11 and thought about how Granny Mabel wouldn't be taking a switch to her or anyone else anymore. Momma's boyfriend, Teddy, had shot Granny Mabel when Pearlie was

14. He came home drunk and Granny Mabel had told him to get his feet off her table. It was Granny Mabel's apartment and she didn't like Teddy or drink.

Teddy didn't say a thing, except "Why just don't you shut up, bitch," and then shot Granny Mabel in the head and fell back down on the couch to watch the Braves game. Pearlie remembered her Momma screaming, the police showing up and rousting Teddy from the couch, and the coroner trussing up Granny Mabel's poor body in what looked like an extra heavy duty Hefty bag with a zipper.

Pearlie missed her Granny Mabel. Her Momma had never talked much after that and just went to work at the Holiday Inn and came home every night to sit in front of the TV.

At first Pearlie tried to get her Momma to talk to her about school or work, but her Momma just watched the TV and sometimes laughed at the people on it. Pearlie felt like a chair that no one really liked anymore, one that would have been thrown out if anyone had noticed it was even there.

Her sister LeeAnn was already married and had moved out before Teddy shot Granny Mabel so she had no time to talk to Pearlie either, not until Pearlie started hanging out with Downey. Then LeeAnn had a lot to say and none of it good.

"Why you want to get Momma to hate me, LeeAnn?" Pearlie asked one time. "I'm your sister. Don't you care that you get me in trouble?" Pearlie asked her when she had first started going over to Downey's.

LeeAnn snorted at her and said that their Momma had enough trash to clean up during the day and didn't need to be bothered with trash in her house.

So Pearlie just started staying over at Downey's more and more and stopped going to school. She was 16 by then and Downey said he'd take care of her. And he did, 'cept she had to do favors for him every now and then by fucking some "friend" he'd just met and could she help him out? And she did, especially when he would give her some crack.

She giggled again as she began walking up Route 11 towards Downey's. Hell, Downey didn't know it, but she'd even suck old Teddy's dick if she got crack out of it now.

Granny Mabel was dead. Dead wrong. Being good didn't make you right with God and sure didn't make you happy, but crack could. Crack could make you forget, feel nothing but good. Fuck Granny Mabel and her Jesus. When did that white Jesus ever help her or anyone she knew?

So Pearlie wasn't even looking when the old green Buick backed up towards her from the Shell station. She didn't even really feel it hit her knees or even feel the hard pavement when she landed. She looked up at the rusted chrome bumper and half-expected to see it still moving, but it didn't. Instead she saw a pair of old sneakers coming toward her and looked up to see a boy holding his hand out to her, asking if she was ok and gee, he was sorry, he didn't see her.

"I'll call the police and get an ambulance. I have insurance," he said.

Pearlie shook her head and crawled up and said "No, no. I'm fine. Don't call. I just fell. I'm ok." She didn't want the police. The last time she'd seen them she'd spent a month in jail waiting to see a judge and she could remember the withdrawal from no more pipe and her Momma coming over with LeeAnn. No, god please, no police. She couldn't go through that again. She just needed to get to Downey's.

She looked up and frowned and said, "I'm ok. I just need to get down the road to a friend's. I'll be fine."

The boy didn't look real happy, but he said, "Well I can give you a ride. Would that help?"

Pearlie thought about it for a minute. This idiot hadn't got any money. The green Buick was older than the dirty John Deere ball cap he wore. At least she could get a ride to Downey's. She faked a little limp trying for sympathy, though in truth her hip did hurt some.

"That would be fine. It's just a few miles north. That would help a lot."

The boy looked relieved now and came round to the passenger side and held the door open for Pearlie. Damn, she couldn't remember the last time a man had held a door for her. He ran around the front of the car and jumped in and backed up and then pulled out onto Route 11.

She felt a little woozy. Maybe she had hit the ground harder than she thought, but she felt nervous sitting next to this boy that she now saw was actually a man who was probably around the same age as Downey. She became more nervous and just began to go on about her friend Downey and how he'd be so relieved to see her. She glanced out the window and saw that the sky was wrong. The sky was getting dark gray where the sun should have been. They never got weather out of the east. It always came from the west. She saw the Staunton Boulevard intersection whir by. She had told him north, hadn't she?

"I think we're turned around. Downey lives up north on 11, past the Shell station."

He didn't speak.

"Woo, my head hurts something bad. Maybe you should stop here. I'm not feeling so good," she said.

Pearlie didn't see his hand holding the sock of coins as it hit her temple. Fast, like a rattler jumping out of the chicory. She could feel something wet on her ear as her head bounced off the passenger window.

"Oww," she started to say and this time the sock hit her in the face between her nose and mouth. She could see a smile on his face as he put the sock down and drove toward the darkening sky.

She thought about Granny Mabel and thought "I'm sorry. I'm sorry," as she closed her eyes and the sky became completely black.

---

While Pearlie Montgomery was about to disappear forever into the Staunton evening, Pearl Taliaferro was laughing as her sister, Mary, sat across from her singing the *Green Acres* theme song to her. She bit into her fudge birthday cake and giggled.

Outside the storm that would soon envelop Pearlie Montgomery, was throwing rain sideways at the bay window in her parents' kitchen and booming thunder around her home.

Pea thought about the horses and knew that Mr. Dickson would make sure they were bedded down. He slept in the hayloft and he always made sure the horses were fed, watered, groomed and sheltered. At 63, he should have been close to retirement, but he had lived at the farm most of his adult life, working for her grandfather even before her father took over the farm.

Pea doubted he'd ever retire and hadn't a clue as to where he would go if he did. His family used to have a lot of land up towards Renick, just north of Frankford, but through the years it had been sold off piecemeal and the family that was left had moved to the western part of the county to work at Meadow River Lumber decades ago. He was probably the last of the Dicksons and he would probably die there in Frankford, not far from his family's old settlement and be buried in the old Dickson Cemetery up the road.

She speared another piece of the fudge and stuck her tongue out at her sister. She was 20 years old today. She had just finished her sophomore year at William and Mary and her sister had just finished her junior year at Greenbrier East High School. Mary attempted a very bad Eva Gabor accent when she sang "Good-bye city life!"

The two fell into a fit of laughter as Mary finished her off-key song, just as lightning struck outside the kitchen window, hitting the maple tree and sending sparks from the nearby transformer as the power went out in the house.

"Good thing we had a candle lit," Pea said as she rose to get a kerosene lamp from off the kitchen counter.

Power outages seemed to be a constant in the summer months in the Greenbrier Valley and her family had never quite given up on having a kerosene lamp and candles nearby in every room of the house.

Pea looked out the back windows towards the barn and could see a small light coming from the second story hay loft. Mr. Dickson would calm the horses. No need to worry. Everything was fine.

But twelve miles away to the east, things were not fine. Her parents were driving back from The Greenbrier where they had met their friends the Akers for their regular Friday evening supper. As her father came upon the old Caldwell place next to the Greenbrier River where a new bridge was being built, he missed the detour and headed onto the half-finished bridge instead, where the new Volvo station wagon dove over the edge and into the white caps of the final spring melt of snow from the higher elevations that had raised the river high. The weight of the Volvo was too much, and though it floated with logs and debris for a few short miles, it also filled with water as it stopped, jammed against the river bank between two blackthorn locust trees.

Neither of her parents could get the doors open as the water filled the Volvo so quickly that they were found the next morning still wearing their seat belts. Pea and Mary were orphans before Pearlie took her last breath almost two hours away.

---

And as Albert and Emma Taliaferro died, Pearlie Montgomery had a very short time left on this earth before the man would be back. She was naked in a dark, dark room that stank like dirt and rotted wood. She couldn't see anything.

"Shit," she said when she tried to sit up, and found her arms, stretched above her head, would not move. Her legs were heavy, almost numb and impossible to move. She thought about Downey and began to cry.

Fuck him and his fucking pipe. Fuck them all. Oh, God, she thought. I want to go home. I'll be good. I want to go home.

She heard footsteps coming near her and she could hear outside the rain beating against some sort of metal roof. The man was back. He held an oil lamp and sat it down on an old metal box in the corner. He didn't speak. He didn't smile. But he never took his eyes off of her.

"Look, if you want sex. I'll do it. Whatever you want. You don't need to tie my arms. I can make you feel good. Just untie my arms and I'll show you," she said.

He looked at her as if she was somehow not right. He tilted his head from side to side and then turned around and began to remove his clothing.

Maybe, she thought, he just wants a fuck and then I can go. I can do that. Her breathing slowed. A fuck. She could do that. Shit. She'd been doing it for five years now. A fuck was just a fuck.

But when he turned around after undressing, he had a buck knife in his left hand and she began to get afraid again. She'd seen buck knives before. Teddy always had one that he used to throw at the wall sometimes when she'd walk by. She never thought he would hit her, but it always scared her and it made Granny Mabel mad, those holes in her wall. Either way, this boy holding a buck knife over her while he was buck naked made her nervous.

Buck knife and buck naked. She was really nervous and that made her laugh for just a second and that made his face turn ugly. She shouldn't have done that. Oh, lord, he was mad now.

He knelt in front of her and pushed her legs apart. She could barely feel them moving on the dirt. What had he done to her legs? He took the knife and wiped it against her stomach and she realized that she couldn't feel much of anything below the waist.

Oh shit, she thought, this was bad. He started cutting her thighs first. Slow, long strokes like the way a man would move his dick inside her. Then he took the knife and put it inside her and did the same thing. She could see him moving the knife in and out in the same slow movements and while she couldn't feel her bladder or bowels letting go, she could smell the piss and shit and blood.

She began to cry hard and started begging him to please stop, to please let her go. He pulled the knife out of her and began to work on her upper body and when he reached her breasts, she could feel a sharp fire spreading across her chest. She tried twisting away from him and dragging her dead legs, but they wouldn't budge now. She started screaming as loud as she could and he still didn't speak.

He touched her lips with the bloody blade, spit into her face, and then began to hack her body into sections. Oh Granny Mabel, I'm so sorry, she screamed. She didn't pass out until he had removed her toes and had started taking each finger from her hands. Then her mind fell away into the dark stink of the room and she knew no one would ever find her again.

# CHAPTER 3

*March 2010*

Pea was trying to be brave today. She was taking her first steps from what she called her "useless existence". She had driven the one hour trip to Lexington to meet Mary for lunch. When she thought about it, it seemed like such a trivial thing to think of as a first step, but for her, after two years of her self-imposed exile into her "useless existence," it was a big step.

Lexington was one of those small Virginia towns that was almost perfect. If a college town was ever exemplified by the university that kept it alive, it was Lexington and Washington and Lee.

This small town boasted more coffee shops and book shops and quaint inns than many small cities did.

And best of all, she could be anonymous here. Outside of the horse crowd which she avoided, she was unlikely to meet anyone she knew. She was only slightly older than the law students there and so she could blend easily into their environment in her Levis, short black leather trench and sneakers. She had no idea that anyone passing by would see beyond what she thought of as her ordinariness and would see her beauty in the cornflower blue eyes, creamy white skin and thick, straight blonde hair that brushed the shoulders of the black leather coat with a light, hypnotic rhythm.

Pea was completely unaware of how she looked or the effect she had on people. She wanted to lose herself among other people desperately so that no one could see that she was horribly afraid and lonely.

When she walked into Winter's Books and Gifts to look for books on local history and geography, she had no idea that her attempts to blend into the others in the store would lead her into the life of Charles William Thornton, III. She had wondered through the store, picking up books and paying no attention to anyone who surrounded her. She was so used to being alone that the thought that other people were around was almost alien.

And that was when she turned and walked straight into Charles Thornton, knocking the books from her own arms and almost knocking him into a book table at the same time. When she realized her clumsiness, she was mortified. What was she doing here? My God, I must be such an idiot, she thought as she knelt and scrambled to pick up the books that were scattered about the gray green carpeting.

"No, you're not an idiot."

She looked up then and saw Thornton for the first time. Now it was worse. She had been talking aloud, not just thinking. Her face turned deep pink and she just wanted to fade into the shelf behind her.

"I'm so sorry. I wasn't paying attention to what I was doing. I should have seen you. I'm really such a klutz sometimes," she said.

He tilted his head to the side slightly and smiled a small crooked smile. He really didn't look upset and she took a moment to realize just how handsome he really was. Dark, curly hair and deep set brown eyes, with a light ruddiness to his skin told her that he spent time outside as much as he did in, but that crooked smile. That was what she couldn't look away from and it was what made her feel even more that she had acted like a fool wandering through the store without paying attention to the people around her.

What she didn't notice was that her appearance had had an impact on him that was more than just a small accident by a foolish woman. He saw all the things in her that she was unaware of – including a kindness and deep sadness in her eyes that most people never saw. He looked into those blue eyes and could not look away.

He handed her one of the books she had been carrying that somehow had transferred itself to his arms in the collision and his fingers briefly touched the soft underside of the palm of her hand. He realized her hand was trembling slightly and he pulled his hand away gently so as not to frighten her.

"Let me help you with those," he said and picked up the last two books from the floor.

"No, no. I should have watched where I was going. I'm really sorry," she said. She could not look up. This was too hard for her. She should have stayed home at the farm today. This whole trip was such a mistake. What made her think she could do this? She had developed a routine in the past two years that was direct and safe. This was not part of that routine. And as she thought about this, her face flushed and she really felt the room beginning to close in around her.

He saw that she was close to panic and took the books from her hands and sat them down on the table behind him, took her by the elbow and began to lead her from the store. He could see that she was not aware of how fast her breathing was or that her hands were now beyond trembling and that her body was beginning to vibrate with panic.

Pea turned her face upward and looked into his eyes, not sure why she was allowing this stranger to lead her out of the store, but aware only that he would help her, she just had to trust him.

By the time they had walked a half block from the store, she discovered that she could breathe again. She hadn't had a panic attack in quite a while and she was extremely embarrassed that this one had just occurred. She stopped and turned to stare at him. Who was he? Men like him didn't just show up. This was no fairy tale. So who was he?

"Are you ok, now?" he said as he quietly and carefully released her arm. Somewhere deep within him something stirred and he didn't want to let her walk away just yet.

"Yes," she said, bobbing her head a bit and blushing slightly this time.

A wisp of blonde hair fell across her cheek and without thinking he reached up and pushed it behind her ear. She smiled, bent her head and touched her ear.

"I really was an idiot. I don't know why I . . . why I," she paused and took a deep breath and looked up at him. "I'm sorry. Truly," she said and firmly nodded her head and smiled.

He laughed and said, "I'm Trey. Would you like to get a cup of coffee? Maybe we can both get out of this wind now."

She gazed back up the street and felt the sting of the wind against her cheek. Of course. Coffee. They were standing a few feet away from a cafe and the rich aroma of coffee somehow made her calmer. She suddenly wanted to know more about this man who had somehow rescued her from a full blown panic attack in the book store.

"Yes, my heavens. It's freezing out here."

He laughed again and held the door open and she felt herself walking into a new world.

They sat together over coffee and he introduced himself to her again. He was Charles William Thornton, III, known since a child as Trey, lived here in Lexington, but had a farm up near Fort Defiance where his family had lived for what seemed like forever. He was an only child. His parents were dead. His mother died when he was 10 and his father had passed away in 1997. He had no brothers or sisters. He liked Lexington because he loved the school and always found interesting things there.

"Like you," he said and smiled, taking a drink of his double espresso.

She watched him as he talked and listened closely as he described his life. It had been so long since she spent time with anyone that she actually did very little talking. She felt a bit ashamed that because of the panic attack he might have seen just how broken she really was. She glanced out the window for a moment and thought that if someone told her that his life had been so ruined the way hers had been that she'd probably find a good reason to run away and not look back.

He gently touched her fingers and said, "Something out there?"

"Oh, no, sorry. I was just thinking." She took a deep sip of her coffee to avoid his eyes.

"Well, this time I should apologize. I've been talking for an hour about myself and haven't given you a chance to get a word in edgewise."

When he said that they had been sitting there for an hour, she remembered her sister and that she was 45 minutes late for her lunch and she wasn't exactly sure where the restaurant was where they were to meet. She had planned on giving herself at least a half hour to find it after buying her books. Now here she sat with no books and no idea where Yung China Garden even was.

She stood quickly and said, "I've got to leave. I didn't realize the time. My sister is probably sending out people to find me. Good heavens, I was supposed to meet her almost an hour ago."

She pulled on her leather coat and threw her scarf around her neck.

"Thank you so much for the coffee and . . ."

He stood and said, "No problem. Well, maybe one. You haven't told me your name." That smile again.

"Pea. Pea Taliaferro," and she held her hand out to shake his. He reached across the table and took her now gloved hand in his and laughed.

"Miss Pea, I am most pleased to make your acquaintance." His brown eyes crinkled slightly as he smiled. His eyes were just a shade lighter than his curly chestnut hair.

"I have a small request," he said. "If you find yourself in Lexington again soon, I'd like to offer you a proper meal and I promise not to monopolize the conversation next time."

She paused again. Did she dare do this? God, he was so nice and it felt good to talk to someone new again.

"I'd like that, too."

"What about Friday?"

She nodded her assent as she opened the door.

"Then I'll meet you at Winter's on Friday at 5 o'clock and take you to a wonderful little Italian restaurant here in town for an early supper."

"Yes. Friday. Winter's. Five o'clock," and she moved out the door and headed back up the street in search of Yung's and her sister.

He walked out after her and watched her walk up the hill. He felt good inside. Warm. He hadn't felt that way in a very, very long time. He turned and as he walked down the hill he thought, yes, this could be very good.

# CHAPTER 4

Mary had not sent out the cavalry after her - yet. But she was starting to get very concerned just as Pea appeared through the door and found her way to the table. Pea was breathless as she removed her jacket, scarf and gloves.

"Did you get lost in Winter's?" Mary wryly commented.

Her sister's proclivity to lose herself in books was a nuisance she had recognized from an early age and had never really liked.

Pea sat down and huffed. "No. I did not. Just because you don't like something beyond West Law means that the rest of us don't either."

"Well, where the hell have you been? It's not like you can get lost in Lexington and besides, I'm hungry." Mary picked up the menu and built a red wall between them while reading it.

"What do you want? Oh, let me guess. Chicken egg foo yung. No 'shrooms."

She peaked over the top of the menu to see if her sister was going to pout or grimace. She was so surprised by the smile on Pea's face that she dropped the menu and looked at her sister intently.

"What the hell is up with you?"

Pea sighed quietly and smiled again. "I met someone at Winter's. Well, actually, I almost knocked him down." She thought about Trey's smile and stopped for a minute.

"And?" Mary asked.

"Oh, well, he's from here, but has a farm up above Staunton near the old Augusta Military Academy, is a few years older than me, raises cattle, is single, never married, no children. Oh! And he's an orphan, or so to speak." Pea was rattling off everything Trey had talked about for almost an hour in just a few sentences.

"Wait," Mary interrupted. "Go back. You knocked him down and he told you all this?"

"No," Pea perused the almost empty room. She really was late.

"Let's order and I'll spill everything," she said and picked up her menu. That was when she noticed the third place setting.

"Is someone else here?" She wasn't sure she wanted to share any of this with anyone else right now.

"Uh, no. Not now," Mary said and began to study her own menu again.

"What do you mean 'Not now'?"

Now Mary was beginning to get irritated again. She knew this whole trip had been hard for her sister to make and she knew that the past few years had taken their toll on Pea, but Mary wanted to move past this and Pea's reticence sometimes made her impatient.

"A friend of mine was going to eat with us. I wanted you to meet him, but you never showed up and he had a class."

"I'm sorry, Ree. Truly, I . . ."

Before Pea could continue, Mary stopped her. "Will you please stop apologizing and saying 'truly'? It's irritating as hell."

Pea looked across the table at her sister. Mary's auburn hair was pulled into a tight knot at the back of her neck and it made her appear more severe, which was ironic in that her sister was the most extroverted person she had ever met. Pea guessed that it was Mary's idea of how a serious law student should look. The ribbed navy turtleneck didn't help, but it did accentuate her sister's beautiful form.

She took Mary's hand in hers and said, "Don't be cross. Please. I met someone really nice today and it was wonderful. Be happy with me."

Mary sighed and suddenly smacked the back of Pea's hand. "Don't make me wait. I worry."

"And I wanted you to meet Joseph."

"Joseph?"

"Yes, Joseph. Pea, he's a really good man. I wanted you two to meet. And you were late so he had to leave and I . . ."

A waiter appeared at the table, placed two glasses of water before them and then waited, pen poised above an order pad. Pea suddenly wondered if he would write their order in Chinese characters or English. As Mary ordered, Pea could see him write numbers instead and she wondered why she always noticed the most trivial things and forgot the more important things, such as a tightened bridle strap.

She could feel the tears about to start and pushed them back. Not today. She pushed everything to the back of her mind and ordered the predicted meal. Mary was right about one thing. She was consistent about food.

Pea related the tale of Trey to Mary, not leaving out any details. Her sister listened as intently as she would have listened to a future client. Pea could see the questions forming with each detail she gave so she left nothing aside. She didn't want to be interrogated and she wanted her sister to see that she was happier than she had been in years.

Mary had few questions other than how Pea felt about everything. She didn't tell Pea that she was going to make sure that this Charles Thornton wasn't going to turn into another Manley Montgomery. She knew her sister couldn't survive that. Why Pea couldn't just see several men before falling under just one man's sway she never understood.

And, Mary had her own secrets she had planned on telling Pea today. Had Charles Thornton changed that? She decided no, he hadn't. But she was still going to find out if the basics of this guy's story were true before her sister could get hurt again and she knew Joseph would help.

And there was the big question. How was Pea going to react? Mary set her chin on her fists and breathed deeply.

"Pea, I need to tell you some things, too."

"Sure, go ahead," Pea said as she stirred the tea the waiter had brought to the table while she had told Mary about Trey.

"I've been seeing Joseph for a few months now. He's here as a guest lecturer in the undergraduate psychology course."

"Guest lecturer? What course?" Pea furrowed her brow.

"Stop that, Pea. Don't start the big sister shit. Just listen and . . . be happy just like you asked me to be."

Pea nodded her understanding and sipped her tea and waited for her sister to continue.

"He's ex-FBI. Profiler. He's giving a series of lectures on the forensic psychology of profiling techniques of serial and spree killers. He's also 45."

There. It was out. Their age difference was what worried Mary the most about how Pea would react. Almost 20 years was a rather large gap, but Mary didn't care. She thought she might be falling in love with Joseph and she hadn't thought she'd ever have time for that. She knew she would certainly never allow herself to be ruled by a man the way Manley had ruled Pea. Wow, she suddenly thought. Manley had hit them both harder than she had realized.

She believed that she had stopped trusting men because she had believed Manley's lies almost as much as her sister had. It was only when she started seeing Manley around campus with a doctoral student that she saw him for the lying bastard that he was.

Even then she couldn't tell Pea what she knew because Pea was so insistent that they had true love. After Alicia's death, Mary knew the real Manley would come out. And he did. He saw her one day in front of the library after embracing the unnamed doctoral student who headed off from him into the library. He told her that Pea wasn't happy and it was making everything hard for them. Could Mary convince Pea to sell the farm and move to Louisiana? They could make a new start there. No bad memories.

Mary had been so disgusted by him. She had just caught him with another woman other than her sister and he had the nerve to ask her to ask her sister to sell the one thing that was keeping her going.

"No," she said and started to walk away from the library when he grabbed her arm.

"You're not going to tell Pea anything stupid, are you?"

She had wanted to spit in his face, but she jerked her arm away from him.

"Leave me alone you bastard. Pea deserves so much better than you."

She ran across the grass toward her dorm, leaving him standing on the gray limestone steps of the library. She never told Pea about it. Not even after Pea did find out about his cheating and lying.

When he took the $150,000, he left and Mary didn't see the need to make her sister's pain any worse. If he had tried to take the farm from Pea, if he had tried to take her sister's money, he would have to face her, but he didn't. He slithered back to

Louisiana and his "Mama" and Mary had hoped that he had drowned in some swamp down there.

"Sorry," Pea said, bringing Mary back into the present.

"It's ok. I just wanted you to meet him. He's an incredible man and,"

"And you're in love?" Pea finished her sentence.

"Maybe. Yes. Yeah, I think so." Mary grinned and dug into her General Tsao's chicken. God, she was starving. All this had made her ravenous.

"I'd like to meet him soon, maybe later this afternoon?" Pea asked.

"Sure. I think his lecture is over at three. We could go over to Savage. He should still be there."

"Then let's finish and get out of here so you can introduce me to your Mr. Right."

They both laughed and Pea raised her hand to get their ticket from the waiter.

# CHAPTER 5

Joseph Hallett was unhooking his laptop from the projector when Pea and Mary came into the lecture hall. The upper level was still dim and at first he thought it was a returning coed coming to ask him more questions about John Wayne Gacy.

Why were they always so fascinated by the clown? He shook his head and turned to continue packing.

"I need a Special Agent's help" He started to laugh when he heard Mary's familiar voice.

"And just what help could I render such a delic . . ."

He stopped immediately when he saw she was not alone as she descended the stairs to the stage. His slightly balding scalp looked almost as red as his face. Mary knew better than to bring someone in here, he thought. He grimaced and turned back to the projector.

He shook his head as if shaking off the worry of her bringing someone here. He saw himself as a little bit pudgy, balding, and only slightly interesting looking middle-aged man with dark straw colored hair. But Mary. What a wonder she was to him. She made him feel tall and strong, like Charles Atlas in the ads on the back of the comic books he had read when he was young. Not the geeky guy who studied people, but like a Special Agent who chased people down in fantastic car chases.

So he really had trouble being even slightly angry with her. She had no idea how much in love with her he was. He had never been a loquacious man, but sometimes she made him so devoid of words that it surprised him. He could not believe that she had even wanted to talk with him, much less make love to him.

He reddened again and coughed. "Mary, how nice to see you."

Pretense. Two hours ago he had kissed her goodbye at Yung's before his class.

Mary touched the shoulder of the woman standing next to her. The blonde woman was older than he had thought. And he also thought probably shyer than he, if that were possible.

"This is my sister, Pea, or I should say Pearl."

Pea held out her hand to the short man standing in front of them. She could sense his embarrassment.

"Pea. Everyone calls me Pea."

But Joseph instantly knew exactly who she was. Mary had told him Pea's whole story. Actually, their whole story. He had come to think of Pea as a virtual recluse over in Greenbrier County after her daughter's death and her divorce and he hadn't been really expecting her to appear at lunch. He saw that Pea was as beautiful as the pictures Mary kept around her apartment, but in person, her eyes made him think that she might also be one of the saddest people he had ever encountered.

"Pea, I'm glad to meet you. We, uh, I had hoped to meet you at lunch, but Mary thought maybe something had come up. I'm sorry I couldn't stay."

"My mistake. I lost track of time at Winter's and by the time I found the restaurant I was very late."

She started to apologize and remembered her sister's earlier rebuke and stopped herself. What the hell was wrong with apologizing, she had asked her sister once?

"Because you do it all the time and often to people who should be apologizing to you." Mary had told her. "I love you, but you've got to stop being so nice. Toughen up a little."

Joseph picked up his laptop case and looked at both of them. The family resemblance was evident in their features, but that was as far it went. For every bit of Mary's strength, he thought he saw in Pea a quiet shyness and maybe fear. This was a woman who was badly hurt, maybe so badly hurt that she might always be this way. Pea seemed the opposite of Mary. Where Mary took adversity and turned it into her own new course, her sister had retreated into a past that he knew had held nothing but heartbreak.

"Pea was going to come over to my place for coffee before driving back. Would you like to come with?" Mary asked.

Joseph hesitated. He liked it here, but upon his arrival there, the department chairman had informed him that the ethics code was very strictly enforced. No fraternizing with students. So just walking across campus with her was a risk.

What the hell. He only had a few months left before he went back home to Fairfax. And Mary would be gone by then, clerking somewhere, making her presence in the legal world. She would either be snatched up by a great law firm or end up as a political aide before following her own political ambitions. The world was open to her in a way that she had no idea how it could be. But he knew. At his age and with his experience, he could see the ones who won and the ones who became drudges in a horrible system. Mary would never be a drudge. She mowed through obstacles like a reaper through field of hay. Nothing stopped her. Retreat was not a word in her vocabulary.

So, what the hell. She didn't know it, but he would have followed her anywhere. I am pathetic, he thought. The 98 pound weakling when she asked him for something. One word and he said yes.

"Uh, sure. Did you drive or walk?"

"Walked."

Of course. Mary walked everywhere, her white iPod ear buds hanging down the front of her shirt, Coldplay or Adele playing as she briskly walked by buildings and people. He shook his head. She really never stopped.

"What's wrong?" she asked.

"Nothing. Long afternoon. Same damn stupid questions."

"Tell me," he asked as they were leaving Savage, "why are women so fascinated by John Wayne Gacy? I would have thought Bundy would be the one they'd want to know about. But no, it's always Gacy."

Mary shook her head. "I don't know."

"Perhaps because Gacy, the man's man, and Gacy, the homosexual killer, is a difficult distinction for them to grasp," Pea said as they descended the steps outside Savage Hall.

Joseph's eyebrows rose slightly. Not what he expected. Mary's sister might be quiet and even fearful, but there was much more to her than he had initially thought.

"You could be right. Gacy, the contractor and man of the community, was a real contrast to Gacy, the murderer."

They walked on in silence for a while when Pea spoke up again.

"Did you ever meet Gacy?"

Joseph shook his head no.

"He was fairly close to execution by the time I was coming up. But he was a nasty piece of work."

"I've met some really twisted people in my life. Mostly men, but sometimes women. All of them both sick in much the same way, but their methodology and causality always a bit different," he continued.

As they walked, he noticed the chairman of the department exiting the library. The chairman watched them, but he neither smiled nor even nodded as they passed.

Well, Joseph thought, I guess I'll be hearing about this in the next week or so. Officious jerk. Browning, the chairman, hadn't spent a single hour in the field doing actually work, but he could move faculty members around like men on a chess board. How had he ever made chair? But Joseph knew the answer to that question – his book on psychology and the justice system, written on the dead bodies of real law enforcement officers.

Joseph hoped that the expensive, gray Brooks Brother suit the chairman wore would split when he sat his fat ass down at his ostentatious desk in his smugly Oxford-want-to-be office.

The chairman was the only faculty member he knew at Washington and Lee who had a spotless desk. Not a paper in sight. Green leather desk pad, dual brass pen holder, and an imitation ormolu clock. No family pictures. Actually, nothing personal at all. And definitely no student papers to be graded. Joseph guessed that Lisa, his secretary, kept the paperwork in carefully organized drawers. She seemed to be a nice woman, but he wouldn't have wished her job on anyone.

"Ladies, let's move along a bit faster. I believe someone is casting a very disapproving eye this way," he said, placing his hand behind Mary's back to try and usher her forward.

But, of course, she stopped completely and stared at Chairman Browning and then she waved and smiled, which completely took Browning by surprise and Joseph was just as surprised to see Browning flush, then wave and head back toward the library doors.

"Mary, one of these days, you're going to stir up a hornet's nest," Joseph laughed.

"Oh, I like to stir things up, especially for pricks like him. Don't worry. I know his secrets, too," she smiled and began to move on.

Pea, slightly confused by the whole incident, watched Browning enter the building and then she caught up to Mary and Joseph. After a few minutes, she spoke to Joseph.

"Joseph, I was wondering, well, I know this will sound stupid, but what are the odds of a serial killer in an area like this?"

Joseph hesitated for a minute, wondering why she asked, but then shrugged it off as an attempt to make conversation.

Later as they drank their coffee at Mary's apartment, he asked Pea why she had asked him the question. When she told him about Pearl Montgomery, he was surprised again by her intuition.

"What makes you think she was murdered, especially by a serial killer?"

Pea paused for a moment and looked around her sister's apartment. Furnished with some pieces from their parents' home and some new, it felt comfortable to her. And Joseph was just as Mary had described him – friendly, open and genuinely sincere.

Pea suddenly realized by their seating in the room and how relaxed he was that he spent as much time here as Mary did and she smiled. She was glad her sister was happy. She just hoped that Joseph wouldn't get lost in the wind her sister left as she flew through a place.

"I, well, I did a little more research and found that other women have disappeared since then, all of them African American, most of them either involved in drugs or prostitution or both, and all of them have been from between Staunton and Lexington."

Joseph sat his cup down. Now she definitely had surprised him. This was new. He didn't think anyone was working on anything like this. He didn't think anyone had even made a connection, if one was to be made.

"How many women have disappeared?"

"Twelve," Pea said.

# CHAPTER 6

"Twelve?" Joseph was stunned for a moment. That large a number was usually caught by someone.

"Yes, twelve. I found the reference to Pearl because of the coincidences with our names, ages, and that she disappeared on my birthday. Then I found a few other stories about the other women."

Pea paused for a moment, wandering if she sounded absurdly ignorant, but Mary broke the silence.

"When did you find this?"

"I'm a bit embarrassed. I did an internet search on my name, hoping to see something about the stables. Instead of me, the missing Pearl came up first. I started reading about her and there were related news stories about the cases. Only one story from last year even tried to tie some of the disappearances together and that was when they thought they had caught someone responsible for one of the dead women."

Joseph leaned forward. He had heard nothing about this and someone at the Bureau would have mentioned it to him, especially knowing that he was coming here to teach for the year.

"Are all the women missing or have bodies been found?" he asked.

"Well, Pearl and at least four women have never been found. Three bodies were found within a mile's distance on the Jackson River, two of them I can't remember, and I think three were found in buried graves near Goshen."

Joseph was removing his laptop from its case as she talked.

"Could you retrace how you found the stories? I'd like to read a little more about this," he asked.

Mary sat her cup on the table. She did not want Joseph's first introduction to Pea to center around a serial killer. This was not how she had wanted to spend the afternoon and she wasn't too happy that Pea seemed almost obsessed with this coincidence.

"Seriously," she said, "Don't you think this is just a line of coincidences? I mean, surely the police or FBI would have seen a pattern before Pea?"

Joseph was watching Pea type in the search terms and spoke to Mary without looking.

"It's completely possible that it's been missed. It happens more than law enforcement would ever like to admit. Sometimes the families are the ones who see the pattern first. Sometimes no one ever sees a pattern, and, unfortunately, sometimes the police just don't have the manpower or time to pursue something that as you said could be coincidence."

Mary moved from the arm of the chair where Joseph sat to kneeling next to the coffee table in front of him.

"Joseph. This just doesn't make sense," she said, stressing the word "sense". She was trying to get him to back off the topic with Pea. She didn't want him encouraging Pea on this search. She was afraid that Pea, in her absence of a reason to move forward, would latch onto something that would lead her into more frustration and pain.

He looked up from the computer screen into Mary's eyes and saw that she was trying to tell him to back off. He thought about it for a minute and then decided he could always check out the information without involving Pea.

"You know, I've got a ton of papers to read this evening, Pea. Could I look over this stuff later?"

Pea sat back on the couch, a bit confused. He had seemed interested. Maybe she was wrong about all of it. Then she saw Mary's face and knew that this wasn't the best time to talk about this.

"Yeah, no problem," she replied and noticed the light beginning to dim outside. "Wow. It's starting to get late and I've got a long drive home."

She stood and went to get her coat. Joseph looked to Mary and then leaned back into the armchair, placing two fingers and thumb to his temple. He knew Mary was worried, but he could also see that in some strange way, this "mystery" had meant something to Pea that was giving her something to think about other than a dead child and unfaithful husband.

And when he leaned back, Mary saw her mistake as well.

Damn, she thought.

"Pea, why not stay here tonight? Maybe we can find out some more information about your new friend?" She smiled and moved to her sister.

Pea returned Mary's smile and looked over to Joseph in the armchair. They were together and she was out of place there. Home was where she needed to go and this wasn't home.

"No, Ree, I've got to get home and get the dogs and horses taken care of before it gets too late. I'll be back later in the week. Maybe we can get together then."

She gathered the rest of her stuff together and opened the door, hugging Mary as she left and whispering quietly into Mary's ear, "I like him. You were right. He's a good guy. A really good one."

Mary bent her head against Pea's shoulder and bit her lip not to cry, then raised her face and smiled.

"Thanks, Pea. Love you. Be careful driving home. Call me later, ok?"

"Will do," Pea nodded and closed the door behind her.

# CHAPTER 7

Mary turned back to Joseph, and then crossed the room to throw herself onto the couch.

"I just screwed up, didn't I?"

Joseph reached over and took her hand.

"No, but Pea needs to get away from that farm. And while she shouldn't be chasing something like this, it's good to see she's interested in something beyond her own past."

Mary tilted her head up to look at him. "Do you think she has found something here?"

He shrugged. "I honestly don't know. I need to look at what she's been reading. Twelve women. That's a lot of women to go missing, with commonalities in their ages, their race, and their social status. It may be more than just coincidences."

He stood up and gathered the coffee cups to take to the kitchen.

"Rural disappearances are the more difficult to piece together when they occur over a wider region and a longer time between episodes," he said.

Mary was sitting up now, listening intently.

"Then again," he said, "Pea could need to find something where nothing is. From what you've told me about her, I think she's lonely and that maybe more than anything else that she needs something beyond what she has now,"

While he took the cups into the kitchen, Mary sighed. She wanted so much to make things better for Pea. That god damned bastard. Everything started going wrong the summer Pea brought him home. It was as if he was the worst bad luck charm they had ever found.

All he had done was destroy Pea, day by day, from the morning after her birthday. First the fake concern, then the lies, the infidelity, the constant badgering to sell the farm, and finally the blame he beat Pea with every chance he had for Alicia's death. And Mary knew that was just one more method of trying to get her to sell the farm.

She had heard Manley speaking with his mother once that summer after her parents had died. He had told Laura to just be patient. He would get things "taken care of" and would be coming back sooner than he had planned.

At the time Mary hadn't thought anything more of it than Manley planning to go home to visit, but later she realized he had been talking about his plan to remove Pea from her home and get her and her money under his complete control.

And he had almost succeeded. If Pea hadn't become pregnant so quickly, he might have gotten her away from the farm. But Alicia had changed his plans. Alicia had changed everything, including Pea.

Pea was the mom that their own mother had been. Loving, attentive, devoted, her child always coming first in Pea's life. Manley did not like being relegated to second place in Pea's life and he certainly hadn't liked the change in his plans. Mary wondered if the infidelity had started then or if it had been a constant thing. Had Pea been just a cash cow for him?

Pea didn't know it, but after Alicia's death and Mary's discovery of Manley's infidelity, Mary had hired a private investigator to check into Manley's life – finances, family, possible girlfriends, everything. And the investigator had found all she needed.

Manley's family was broke and nearly bankrupt. His family was a concoction of what his mother thought a southern aristocratic family should be, taken from bad romance novels and a Tennessee Williams play here and there. Laura had grown up dirt poor with her "beloved" daddy nothing but a mean and mostly absent drunk. Her husband, while rich only in worthless Louisiana acreage and an old southern surname, wasn't much better.

Laura had spent her entire adult life trying to mold Manley into that ridiculously extinct idea of a southern gentleman of leisure by putting him into schools where he could make contacts that would bring them the wealth she needed to be the person she thought she was instead of the cracker she really was.

Mary had been ready to give all that information to Pea when Pea had surprised her by throwing the bastard out first.

"Stop it."

Mary broke from her fugue and found Joseph standing over her.

"You couldn't and can't change what happened. He was a sociopath and he was a very talented one, at that," he said.

How he could know what she was thinking often amazed her. What she didn't know was that he could see the dark storm clouds in her eyes every time she began to brood about what he had come to call the "Manley" situation.

"But, why didn't I see it?" she asked.

He sat down next to her on the chintz sofa and she stretched her arms out, twining them into his arms. She lightly stroked his arm where his shirt sleeves were rolled up. In the window behind the couch, the daylight was fading, the once gray day now turning slightly yellow as the sun began to set beyond the hills around Lexington.

"I should have seen it. I should have told her the first time I saw him with someone else. I should have . . ."

Joseph placed his hands on her cheeks, using his thumbs to wipe away the tears that threatened to spill down her face. Her auburn hair shone in the yellowing light.

"You couldn't have known anymore than she had. You've got to stop blaming yourself. Just be there for her."

She touched his lips with her fingers.

"I love you," she said and leaned into his chest, the crisp, blue oxford cloth separating her face from his warm skin. "I'm so lucky to have you here." And she wrapped her arms around his chest.

No, he thought. Not as lucky as I am right now. God, he hoped his luck would hold out and he hugged her tightly to him.

He rose and led her toward the bedroom and she followed, her right hand entwined with his left hand. He sat upon the bed before her, watching the changing weather of her face. He began to undress her slowly, kissing the smooth silkiness of her belly as he removed the navy turtleneck and unzipped her jeans.

She leaned into him, falling against him on the plush comforter, the woven Jacobean tapestry folding against them both as they struggled out of the rest of their clothing. She rested her head against his shoulder and kissed it, her hair falling forward against him. She moved her lips along his neck and ever upward toward his lips as her arms found their way around his body.

In the short six months that they had been together, she had memorized his body, knowing the places that he moaned in a whisper as she touched and kissed them.

When their clothes lay upon the bottom of the bed and on the Aubusson rug beneath her bed, she sat up above him and paused to look into his large, pale blue eyes.

"I do love you, Joseph."

He sat up and brought her chest against his face, kissing her breasts, burying his face between them, trying not to think of a future without her, trying to keep hope alive for just this moment. And she, almost knowing the questions in his own heart, lifted his face upward to hers.

"Will you leave me in May?" she asked. "I can't think of that. Please tell me we'll be together. I need to know. I can't . . . I can't lose you."

Her words left him breathless. God, he would never leave her, but he was too afraid to ask her the same.

Instead, he said, "I will always love you. Always."

He brought her down to the bed and rolled her onto her back and entered her, moving slowly, deeply, feeling her thighs wrap around his as their bodies became more urgent to hold tight against the storms in their hearts.

"Joseph, I won't leave you, no matter what our future brings. Please tell me you won't leave me. I need to hear you say it. Don't make me beg."

How could she not know, he wondered. He kissed her cheeks and leaned his forehead against her beautiful porcelain skin.

"I will never leave you. I love you," he said and laid his face against her auburn hair spread across the pillows, falling into her, loving her, their breath joining rhythmically as they made love long into the early evening.

# CHAPTER 8

Pea used the drive back to the farm to think about the events of the day. First, the surprise of Mary's love for the man who was so different from her beyond age and spirit. Joseph was such an unlikely man for her and yet Pea couldn't help feeling that in their own unusual way, they fit perfectly together.

Besides, it wasn't as if she could ever be called any sort of expert on love. Everything she had thought that was true about love had been proven glaringly and painfully wrong. She had thought she had true love and she had had nothing except her own thoughts. It was if she had held a seashell to her ear and while hearing her own heart echoing into the shell, she had thought she had heard his heart there, too.

What a stupid, naïve fool I was, she thought. And the only good thing that had come from her self delusion had been that beautiful auburn haired child whom she had let die. That was a blame that Manley had rightly laid at her door. For two years she had gone over those last few moments before Alicia rode away from her. Had she secured Alicia's helmet? Were the reins set firmly? Was Alicia ready to do this? Yes, to all those questions.

But no to the question that haunted her constantly. She could not remember tightening the saddle strap beneath the palomino's belly. And that failure had probably cost her the life of her beautiful little girl.

Her eyes began to sting with hot tears. Instead of really seeing I-64 in front of her, she saw instead the too still body of her daughter on the ground, the horse running away, the small red coat and black helmet in relief against the light tan clay of the track. One-half lap and Alicia was gone.

Without realizing that she had run across the field, she had found herself kneeling next to Alicia, whispering as she cried, "Wake up baby. Sit up. It's ok. Mommy's here. Alicia, open your eyes for Mommy. Open your eyes now. Mommy's here."

Manley had stood over them, not speaking, and then everything had happened at once. The EMTs, the air lift to UVA, the doctor looking down as he told them Alicia wasn't going to wake up, and

Mary there, holding her, keeping her from tipping over onto the pink and gray tiled floor of the emergency room hallway and then leading her home, with Manley silently following them into the back seat of Mary's little Honda.

Pea wiped her eyes and shook off the view from that night, finding the road in front of her had darkened from twilight to night. She flicked on her headlights and thought about the animals. Mr. Dickson, now 77, would have seen to feeding them. She sighed as she watched the brown deadened winter trees along the way. The 55 mile an hour speed limit on I-64 through Virginia made the trip feel interminable.

After a while she found her breathing returning to a more normal rhythm, feeling the pain lifting a bit and she thought about Charles Thornton. Did she want to see him again? Could she go through that particular dance again? It almost seemed impossible, but she remembered the way his eyes crinkled at the corner as he smiled, the way he had led her out of the bookstore. He had to have known that she had had a panic attack and yet he hadn't said one word about it. He had treated her normally, as if she were someone he just wanted to meet and talk to about everyday things.

Did she dare meet him Friday? Again, his smile appeared in her thoughts and she smiled to herself, even as she was wiping the tears away from her face. Yes, she wanted to see him again. She needed to see him. She needed someone in her life, suddenly thinking about Mary and Joseph. She was almost jealous of them. They fit. They fit so well. And she wanted to fit with someone, really fit, hear their hearts and not just an echo of her own heart, especially with someone she could trust. And she thought she might be able to trust Charles Thornton.

As she drove past Clifton Forge, she thought about the women she had wanted to talk to Joseph about. Well, that wasn't going to be easy with Mary. Mary had so obviously disapproved of the questions and Pea's pursuit of what had really happened to those twelve women.

I'm not giving up on them, she thought. Why she felt she had to do this, she wasn't quite sure. Maybe it was Pearl Montgomery, the other woman with her name. Maybe it was the whole coincidence of Pearl's disappearance and how the tragedies had begun then in her own life as well. There have to be some answers out there as to why their deaths and disappearances had gone unnoticed by most.

Then she thought of Thomas Washington. Washington, according to the *Staunton Dispatch*, had been the leading suspect in their deaths because his DNA had been found on one of the bodies – that of Shawnette Davis, a young coed at Mary Baldwin whom he said he had been seeing for several months.

She didn't remember whether the paper had gone into too much detail about Washington's relationship with Shawnette, but just before he was about to be bound over to the grand jury, another body was found in close proximity to Shawnette's with the same torture signature. With no evidence linking him to the other body, he had been released from jail.

Pea wondered if she could locate Washington and talk to him. He had been living in Staunton when Shawnette had died, working as a welder for a company called Smith or something like that. She'd have to recheck the newspaper for the exact name. If she found that he had remained in Staunton, she might be able to talk to him and find out if the police or he knew anything more about the twelve women.

She considered for a moment that seeking Washington out might be truly a stupid thing to do if he were responsible for Shawnette's death, but somehow, with some weird clarity of intuition, she didn't think he was responsible. She thought he might be an innocent man caught up in events beyond his control.

Events beyond his control. She could understand that.

The last twelve years had seemed to be nothing but a series of events beyond her control.

By the time she reached the Lewisburg exit and headed north toward the farm, she had made some decisions about what she would be doing this week. First, she would locate Washington this week and then Friday leave very early that morning to go to talk to him. If she timed everything just right, she would be able to see Washington, possibly check the *Staunton Dispatch* newspaper morgue for any more information about the twelve women, and still drive back to Lexington to meet Charles Thornton at Winter's in time to eat with him at what he had called that "wonderful little Italian restaurant."

As she parked her car behind the house, she had her plan firmly in hand and exited the car to head out to the stable. As she entered the barn, the palomino in the first stall came to her and lowered his head to allow her to stroke his long face.

It's not your fault, Blondie, she sighed. You didn't know the saddle wasn't fastened securely or that an idiot would throw a firecracker behind the bleachers on the far side of the track.

Pea lay her cheek against the horse and let her tears fall. It wasn't his fault. It wasn't his fault.

# CHAPTER 9

*June 1999*

He had been watching Mattie Sue Caldwell for several weeks now. Her routine rarely changed, which was both a good and bad thing for him. The chances of his being seen were heightened, but then that risk also heightened his desire to take her.

She had found herself a niche at the I-81 truck stop parking lot at Waynesboro where every night she moved between the trucks, sometimes picking up a trick, sometimes just waiting in boredom.

He parked across from the truck stop in a small dirt turn-around that seemed rarely used. His car disappeared into the foliage surrounding the spot and he felt somewhat confident that no one, especially the working girls in the parking lot, ever noticed him parked there.

He didn't find Mattie particularly attractive, but he hadn't thought Pearl had been either. They were simply easy to take and mostly disposable. Who paid attention to whores? Certainly no one he knew.

He had decided to use her need for money to bring her to his car. Unless someone tried to pick her up first or if she decided to stand around with some of the other whores, it should be easy to lure her over.

He pulled the dirty John Deere cap down, hiding most of his face and pulled at the itchy label of the black Metallica t-shirt he wore. The legs of his jeans were stained with grease and the Dollar Store sneakers were beginning to separate at the soles. Even if he did run into someone he knew, they wouldn't have recognized him. His disguise was as perfect as his plans and he needed those plans to come together tonight.

He could feel his penis getting hard in his pants as he walked up from behind the trucks toward Mattie who had stopped to adjust the strap on her sandals while leaning against one of the semis.

When she heard his footsteps behind her, she whirled around quickly and then saw that it was just a short, guy, probably looking for one of the girls to relieve his boredom.

"Hell, boy. You scared the shit out of me. Don't be sneaking up behind people like that," she said.

She closed the distance between them and touched his arm. "You lookin' for something sweet, sugar?"

Damn, she hated this part. The asking for money for sex part. She had never liked it, but since she was 17, it had been an easier way of making money than washing toilets in the local Exxon station. She had tried that for two months when she finally got tired of the smell of shit. She left the bucket and mop propped up against the door of the Women's Room and had just walked away. She wasn't cleaning up anyone's shit anymore. It was so much easier just fucking or sucking off one of the truck drivers than ever having to wring out that nasty mop again.

The man nodded and then said, "Could you come over to my car? I'm just parked across the road." He tilted his head in the direction of the Buick in the turn-around.

"Sure, honey. Is that your car there?" She asked as she started walking back toward the old Buick.

She gave a little twist as she walked, hoping he might want more than just a suck. She might be able to get him to do a little something extra if he had the cash.

He walked behind her and let her get in the passenger side on her own. He had removed the dome light in the car so no one would notice them or the car as they opened the doors. He had planned on subduing her the same way he had the woman last year with sock of rolled quarters against her head, but just as he swung the sock forward she turned to see it coming toward her and lifted her hand up to grab at it.

He hadn't been prepared for this and so instead he used his fist, smashing it over and over again into her cheekbone harder than the sock would have. She began to fight him, but he had picked her for her size and even with the futile swipes of her nails against his cheek, he had beaten her into unconsciousness in less than a few minutes.

He got a Kleenex from the back seat and wiped off his face and hand. Fucking cunt. He looked at her slumped down toward the floor of the Buick and could see that her left eye was badly cut, bulging so far from her eye socket that it looked disgusting.

He reached over and plucked the eyeball from her eye socket and tossed it out the window into the bushes. Knowing the local wildlife, especially the turkey buzzards that circled over I-81, it would be gone by the next afternoon and it wasn't like she was going to need it anyway.

He was taking her to his place again and he had everything set up for his fun evening ahead. He felt his dick strain against the denim again as he thought about his plans for the night. Boy, were they going to have some fun tonight.

Mattie woke up in almost the same spot Pearl had struggled to consciousness, but she couldn't see everything and she screamed out when she realized that her eye didn't feel like it was there anymore.

Like Pearl, she started to sit up and saw that her hands were tied about her head, but unlike Pearl, she knew about getting loose from knots. She had to. Some Johns got a little too carried away with the ropes so she had learned to use one very sharp fake nail like a little wedge to wear against and often loosen the ropes anytime she found herself in a place that felt unsafe.

And this place felt all kinds of unsafe. With her one good eye, she could see light coming through the cracks in the floor above her and hear footsteps moving around overhead. Mattie hoped to God that it was just the one piss ant she was going to have to handle. More than him would be real tricky.

Just as she had her hands free, she started to stand and found her legs refused to cooperate. What the fuck? She lifted her right knee and it fell hard back against the ground. The fucker had given her some kind of spinal block like when she'd had her baby, Darius. Oh fuck, no, she was not going to die in this basement. She frantically looked around for something to use as a weapon and saw a screwdriver on a shelf near the pole where her hands had been tied.

She dragged herself over to the shelf, praying whoever was upstairs wouldn't come down before she could grab it and then move back to the pole. Just as she put her hands behind the pole, she heard a door open and saw the man slowly walking down the wood steps, carrying a lantern in one hand and a knife in the other.

I'm gonna kill you fucker, she thought. Just come on over here a little closer. I've got a little surprise for you. She closed her one good eye and pretended to moan a little.

He seemed to ignore that she was lying across the floor from him, but she didn't know that he saw the dirt on her legs or her skirt had hiked up a little higher than when he had tied her up. Now he could see a bright red thong peeking at the edge of the skirt. He knew she had gotten loose and was trying to think how he was going to handle this. Whatever she had in her hands could hurt him and that was a risk he couldn't take.

He got angry for a moment. Did she think he was stupid? Damn what a stupid whore she was thinking he wouldn't notice that she was filthy or that her arms were slightly slack rather than tight against the pole. He circled around her, giving her wide berth so that he could come up behind her.

That was when she saw that he was onto her and she lunged at him with the screwdriver, but managed only to sink it into the dirt floor.

Shit, shit, shit. She started crying from her remaining eye, thinking that the blood from where her other eye had been was also a tear.

He laughed and kicked her chin hard back against the pole while bending over to grab the screwdriver up.

"You like screwdrivers? We can use it, too," he said.

He grabbed her hands and pulled them behind the pole and stabbed the screwdriver through her palms, her arms now at a safe distance from him.

She screamed louder than she ever had. But she was still angry with this motherfucker.

"You bastard. I'm gonna kill you. I'm gonna get loose from here and fuck you up," she said. She wanted to kick at him or grab at him but both her arms and legs were useless now.

He started laughing and began to undress. He walked over to her and cut her clothes away, the buck knife easily moving through the cloth.

This time before starting his ritual, he kicked her hard in the crotch with the heel of his foot. He could feel her pubis crushing a bit as he removed his foot. Then he knelt before her and began the first cuts, then moving the knife inside her as he had with Pearl.

Mattie couldn't feel it but she watched his every move and knew she wasn't getting away this time. But unlike Pearl, she didn't scream until he cut her nipples off. She had been able to stay quiet till then. She didn't want to give the bastard the satisfaction of hearing her cry out. But when he took her nipples and shoved them into her empty eye socket she did begin to scream. She screamed without stopping, even after he had removed her hands and feet. She was still screaming as she began to pass out as she saw him jerking off in one last hazy gaze. By the time he had finished, she had bled out and was gone.

He stood up and looked over his work. She had really been fun. Now he had to clean up and get her out of there. This was always the boring part for him. He sighed as he removed the screwdriver from her small hands, and smiled for a moment.

Now that screwdriver. That had been inspired. Shame he couldn't have kept her a day or two longer. She had really been fun.

---

The week after Mattie had died, Pea was about to celebrate another momentous event in her life. In less than an hour she would be married to Manley Warren Montgomery. So she sat in her bedroom at her childhood white French provincial desk in a thin, old fashioned nylon slip and could not stop crying.

She could hear the bustle of activity outside her door and knew she had precious few moments before the room would explode into activity, but in those moments she allowed herself to mourn her parents' absence that night. Her mother should be here helping her to dress, tucking her blonde hair up into a French twist, standing behind her as she looked at herself in the mirror in her wedding gown and veil.

And damn, she just needed her father pacing outside the door, waiting for the two of them to exit so he could take her arm and parade her down that aisle one last time as if to say to the world, this is the wonder that God has given us.

Pea lifted a champagne flute from the desk and drained it. She could hear Mary trying to keep Laura at bay, but Pea knew it was a useless endeavor. Laura was going to burst through that door at any second and begin to give her paragraphs full of unwanted and unwarranted advice. Pea didn't realize until that second just how much she disliked Manley's mother. Oh, on the surface everything seemed perfect, but underneath she could see a hatefulness in Laura and knew that Laura not only disliked, but loathed Pea.

Thank God, Laura would be in Louisiana and far from them after tonight. She poured one more small sip into the flute and drank it in.

Well, I might as well get this started, she thought as she wiped her eyes and walked over to unlock the door. And, of course, Laura was the first one through the door, rushing at her in a pale pink Chanel suit. Wonder how much that cost me, Pea thought wryly.

If she didn't love Manley so much, if he weren't so good to her and didn't love her as much, she would have kicked his mother's skinny butt out of her room. She knew Manley had sent Laura a credit card with a $10,000 limit on it with the bills to be sent to him and she knew that Laura had already gone through most of the credit limit, but she pretended it wasn't there for his sake. It was his mother. What could she do?

Thankfully, Mary quickstepped between Laura and Pea, followed by Pea's sorority sister bridesmaids giggling and gossiping. Guess she wasn't the only one who had had an early start on the champagne.

Oh, but thank God for sober Mary, so much like their mother, easily taking control of everything and ushering Laura towards the door, whispering that she needed to be in her seat for Manley and that they'd be downstairs in a jiffy.

Mary locked the door again as Laura left and raised her bouquet in a celebratory gesture, silently mouthing the word "Yes!" as she walked across the room to help Pea into their mother's wedding gown.

"Thanks Ree. I did not need to hear from her right now."

Pea turned to the mirror and for a brief moment saw her mother's proud gaze fade into the image of Mary behind her in the mirror. She was going to cry if she didn't get out of here and find Manley at the end of the aisle.

It was only after her bridesmaids had walked down the aisle in her mother's garden that she stood waiting alone, her father not there. So she was shocked when she looked down the white cloth aisle as she began her trek towards Manley that she thought she might be making a huge mistake.

Every eye in the audience was on her except for him and she saw him look at his mother and wink. Oh God, what was she getting herself into? But instead of listening to her head, she allowed her lonely heart to lead her toward him and buried deep the thought that she was about marry a man who would never love her.

Loneliness could make you do foolish things she would think 12 years later. It certainly had that night.

# CHAPTER 10

*March 2010*

Pea was on the road again driving between Lewisburg and Lexington. It was very early, the sun only having risen a half hour ago, but she wanted to catch Thomas Washington at home before he left for work. She had meticulously planned her day, even allowing for any interruptions that might her delay her meeting Charles Thornton at Winter's. And she wasn't going to miss him. She didn't have a phone number for him or even an address so she had to be at Winter's at 5 o'clock, come hell or high water.

What she hadn't prepared for was that Thomas Washington had no plans of going anywhere that day. At that moment he was lying in bed watching the overhead fan spin in slow circles. The dry cleaner below his apartment kept it like an oven all year long and he ran the fan even in winter.

Shawnette used to tease him about it. He stretched his arm across the void where she used to curl up next to him and found empty air. Sometimes he swore he could smell her perfume in the room or hear her tinkling laughter coming from the kitchen. But she was never there. She was gone and hadn't been found until last summer near the body of another murdered woman.

He rolled over and buried his face in the pillow, pulling his heavily muscled arms against his head so he could try to stop thinking about how she had been tortured before she died. He was on the verge of crying out her name when he heard a soft knocking at the door of the two room apartment.

He sat up on the edge of the bed and rubbed his hand across his head. He pulled on an old pair of work pants and a once white t-shirt over his head and broad chest as he crossed the living room to the door. He opened it to find a tall blonde woman standing at the top of the steep stairs, dressed in a very expensive leather coat and straight black skirt. He raised his eyebrows for a moment as he took in her sudden appearance at his door.

He looked past her for a second to see if someone else was out there, like a cop with a warrant.

"Are you Thomas Washington?" she asked.

He frowned for a moment trying to decide whether to even talk to her. She looked like trouble waiting to happen and he'd had enough of that. "You've got the wrong person, lady," he said and closed the door. But as he walked away, the knocking began again.

He swung the door open and started to tell her to go away, but she started talking fast.

"If you're Thomas Washington, I need to talk to you about Shawnette. Would you let me come in and at least talk to me for a moment?"

Before he could say a word, she had slipped under his arm and into the room.

What the hell?

"What do you want?" he asked.

"If you're a reporter, I got nothing to say to you. If you went to school with Shawnette, then you probably know more than I can tell you, so lady, I really got nothing to say to you. Could you please just leave?"

Pea looked him over and thought that Shawnette had had nothing to fear from this man. Yes, he was tall, very muscular and a very handsome man who could probably have charmed his way into just about any woman's life. But she still didn't feel afraid of him although she had literally forced her way into his home.

Instead of leaving, she sat down on his sofa making him aware that she wasn't going anywhere.

Oh hell, he thought. She was almost as stubborn as Shawnette had been. He definitely wasn't going to get rid of her.

"Lady, I need some coffee. I just got up. Do you want a cup?"

While he fixed the coffee, Pea took off her coat and gloves and looked around the room. For a man, it was surprisingly immaculate, but pictures of Shawnette were everywhere and she stood up and walked over to one on a side table and picked it up and saw Shawnette's incredibly sunny smile.

"Please put that down."

Pea turned to find him standing behind her, holding two cups of coffee.

"I'm sorry. First let me introduce myself. My name is Pea Taliaferro."

She paused for a second. She had rehearsed in the car exactly what she would say, but it didn't sound the same in her head now with Thomas standing before her. Still, without taking a chance to rethink her words, she plowed ahead.

"I think Shawnette was . . . I think Shawnette was the eleventh victim of a serial killer here in the Staunton area."

He fell back into the recliner behind him and gaped at her. He was having trouble processing any of this. Shawnette. Killed by a serial killer? In Staunton? This made no sense. He raised his face up and looked into Pea's eyes.

"Why?" he asked as he sat the cup on the cheap coffee table and closed his eyes. Oh Shawnette, god, no, please. He felt the pain of her death fill him just as strongly as it did when he was first told she was dead by the cops.

Pea sat down on the sofa close to him and placed her hand on his arm.

"I'm so sorry," she said. "I didn't think and I should have. I have a tendency to just blurt things out sometimes. I'm sorry. I know what it's like to lose someone. I'm sorry if I've made it worse."

God, she felt awful. Why hadn't she thought that he would still be mourning Shawnette anymore than she still mourned Alicia?

He pulled his arm away from her hand. Why had he opened the door to this woman? He should have known she would be nothing but trouble for him. He looked closely at her.

"I don't understand what you want. What does this have to do with you?"

Pea took a drink of her coffee and followed it with a deep breath before laying out the story of the 12 murdered women. But this time she had come prepared, pulling out computer printouts of the news stories about all the women and even the story about his arrest and release, slowly going over her theory, point by point.

By the time she finished an hour had passed and she thought about his having to go to work.

"I'm sorry. Have I made you late for work? I just wanted to talk to you about all this before you left for the day."

He curled his lips slightly. "I lost my job when Shawnette died and no one wants to hire me now. I've got nowhere to be this morning."

"Oh, I'm sorry. I thought you were still at Smith's."

"No, they let me go and everyone but you seems to think I'm the one who hurt Shawnette, so, so no one will hire me. I get lots of excuses, but I know they still think I did it," he said. "But I didn't. I loved her, had wanted her to marry me," he stood up and went over to a bookshelf holding a TV and a small collection of books and photographs of Shawnette and him in better days. He took a small black velvet ring box down and handed it to her. "I would never have hurt her. She was my future."

Pea opened the box and saw the tiny diamond and felt so hurt for him. She believed her intuition about him had been right.

"Can you help me?" she asked. "I can't tell you why this matters to me, but there are some coincidences that fit into my life that make no sense. I can't stop thinking about these women and other than you, no one else even seems to care that they're gone."

She handed the box back to him and he opened it to look at the ring again. Shawnette deserved better. He glanced across the coffee table to the pictures of the other women. Shawnette would have said that they deserved better, too.

He held his hand across his forehead, feeling as if a bad headache was coming. Lord this felt bad, but he knew he had to do it.

"I'll help. I don't know how, but I'll try. Shawnette would have wanted that."

Pea smiled at him and said, "Well, tell me about Shawnette first. Where you met, what she was like, where you went, anything that you can remember."

"Lady, I can remember everything. Everything." And he started to tell this odd young woman about his Shawnette.

# CHAPTER 11

"You did what?"

Joseph was in his tiny, windowless faculty office sorting test results when Pea had knocked. There was barely room for one person to maneuver around the desk and the overflowing bookshelves on the other wall, but somehow he had managed to get around the desk and seat her in a chair that must have been in basement storage since Lee had died. He had been pleased to see her again. Mary would be glad to know that she was here. And that was when she told him about her trip to Staunton.

He sat back in the most uncomfortable desk chair he had ever had and just stared at Pea.

"How could you do something so, well, so stupid?" The words left his mouth before he could stop them. Ok, now I've just called the most important person in my lover's life stupid.

Brilliant move, Hallett. Maybe cussing would make it worse.

But Pea seemed unfazed by his outburst. She stared down at the floor for a second and then lifted her chin. Oh, he had seen that chin lift on Mary. Pea was a lot more like Mary than he had ever thought.

"Ok. Sorry. That was rude. But what you did was dangerous. This Washington could be a killer. According to law enforcement, he is the killer of Shawnette Davis. From everything I've read, he did kill her."

Pea puzzled over that for a moment. "You've been checking into the women, haven't you? You believed me."

He sighed. He was never going to get Mary to understand this, but Pea was absolutely right. Twelve African American women had either been murdered or disappeared over the last twelve years. He had used her basic information and had pulled some favors with local law enforcement to get copies of their files. What had stunned him the most was that absolutely no one but this blonde woman with Mary's defiant chin had put it all together. And all because the first victim had had her name.

"Yes, Jesus, Mary's going to kill me over this. If she finds out you went to Washington's apartment, she'll go ballistic on both of us," he said.

"I know," Pea responded. "That's why I came to your office instead of Mary's apartment."

She leaned forward and pulled the sheaf of print-outs from her bag that she had shown Thomas Washington. She put them on his desk, almost daring him to not help.

"This is all I've been able to access on the internet. If you've checked into any of it, you may have more."

Joseph picked up the papers from his desk and leafed through them. He had most of what she had, except for a few things he hadn't come across online.

"I have most of this, but I also have more." He sighed and opened his desk drawer and pulled twelve files from the drawer. "I also have the police reports."

Pea stood and grabbed them up greedily and began to read through them, but he stopped her at the first page of the Pearl Montgomery file, closing it on her hand.

"Pea, there's some very unpleasant stuff here. Some very ugly stuff and some photographs you may not want to see. Let me work on it. I promise to keep you up to date on whatever I find."

She handed the files back to him. "I can take it."

The chin thrust again.

"Have you lost a child, Joseph? If you can live through that, you can take a lot. Besides, I have something that no one had or has had access to."

He stood holding the files to his chest and looked down.

"I'm sorry Pea. I didn't mean to be condescending. I just didn't want you upset, and," he stressed this to her. "What's in these files is very bad. Police officers with years of experience have trouble with stuff like this."

"Police officers with years of experience have ignored these women. We're always being ignored unless our sexuality is the right type or we're the right color or whatever." She was a bit angry with his little lecture.

"Let me tell you what these women, what most women have to endure - groping and dismissal by men as just sexual beings until we get old and then we're eccentric or senile and worst of all, invisible. We're betrayed, we're left alone and no one even looks at us unless we look a certain way. . ."

He stopped her before she could continue. Damn, she was worse than Mary. She wasn't just a hurt woman. She was an angry, hurt woman.

"I understand that Pea. I'm one of the good guys, remember? I just didn't want to . . . oh, hell, I didn't want you hurt and Mary mad at me. And before you start to get upset with me again, remember I believe you, but I know you've had no experience with this kind of sadistic sickness. So, maybe I was being overprotective. It was well intentioned, but . . . I apologize."

Pea sat back down in the chair across from his desk and he retreated back into his chair, the two of them moving into opposite corners like two tired fighters.

"I, we, Thomas and I need your help," she said.

He stared into her eyes and saw that she was going through with this no matter what.

"Are you sure he's not, that he didn't kill Shawnette Davis?"

She smiled at him. She knew then that he was going to help them.

"I'm as sure of that as I am that you love my sister. Am I wrong?"

He ran his hand through his thinning hair, closed his eyes for a moment and then looked at her straightforwardly.

"No, you're not wrong. In fact, you're absolutely right.

Now, he thought, how the hell am I going to tell Mary about this?

Pea rose to leave and then pulled a red cloth book from her bag and handed it to him.

"This might help."

"What is it?" he asked as he took it from her gloved hand.

"It's Shawnette's journal. She was being followed. Read it. She was a very bright woman," and Pea turned to leave him, laughing very quietly with the knowledge that his mouth was agape.

# CHAPTER 12

She was going to arrive at Winter's just a few minutes before five and she stopped to look at her reflection in a window. Why are we always surprised by our own reflections, she wondered. We never expect what we see in windows, even when we've checked everything in a mirror first. Maybe we see ourselves more in windows as others see us rather than as we see ourselves in mirrors.

She shrugged her shoulders slightly and moved on down the hill toward Winter's. Would Charles Thornton be there? Would he even show up? She hoped he would, but a brief moment of anxiety passed through her body.

How can I be so assertive sometimes and so passive when it comes to a man I'm interested in, she thought. I should have been terrified this morning when I knocked on Thomas Washington's door and yet there I went, right into his living room. And yet I'm scared to death to go inside this store.

She looked in the window of the store and saw Thornton standing near a front shelf, turning pages in a book that he didn't seem too interested in. She used that moment to take a long look at him. Ok, he still was very handsome. Her memory about that had been right. Well built. Tall. And somewhat relaxed. He was dressed for dinner. He was wearing a charcoal suit and dark red tie. He put the book back on the shelf and looked at his watch and then out the window to see her standing there. He smiled and she blushed at being caught watching him. They both started towards the door to Winter's, but he was outside and standing in front of her before she reached the door.

"I'm glad you came," he said as he pulled on a Burberry trench coat over his suit. "Are you hungry?"

"Starved," she laughed.

"Then let's get out of here and get some Italian," and he put his arm at the small of her back and led her forward.

As they drove through Lexington in his Celica, they at first sat in an uncomfortable silence. Pea wasn't quite sure what to say. It had been over 12 years since she had been on a date. She started to say "Charles" and he interrupted her.

"Trey. No one's called me Charles since I was in boarding school." He turned to briefly smile as he said this and shifted the Celica's gears.

"Sorry. Where did you go to school?"

He stared at the road ahead as remembering a place he hadn't liked much. "Newport."

"Not a lot of farm boys there," he said.

She dropped the subject. She could imagine that he had might have been miserable there and she didn't want to cause the evening to turn into a disaster before it had even begun.

"Sorry, again. I don't, I haven't been out in a long time. I may have forgotten some of the proper protocol," she said and flashed a small smile his way.

"Don't apologize. I don't go out much either."

He pulled into the parking lot of the restaurant and let the Celica glide easily into place.

"We can learn about this again together."

"No, I really haven't dated. Really."

He got out of the car and opened the door for her, offering his hand, "Let's get some food and you can tell me about Miss Pea. After all, I probably bored you to death at the cafe with my monologue."

The restaurant was intimate and quiet. The small tables were separated with plants and stuccoed half walls that offered privacy. The maitre d' knew Trey immediately and without pause led them to a very private corner next to a window that overlooked a small garden.

Trey saw that Pea had noticed the little garden which was just beginning its spring growth again.

"They grow their own herbs here and make all their pasta to order. The food really is delicious."

Pea had removed her jacket and gloves and hoped that the v-neck cashmere sweater with a pearl choker she wore wasn't too casual or revealing. She had taken the time to put her hair into a French twist before meeting him and she patted the back of her head to make sure no stray wisps were escaping.

He watched her as she performed each movement, admiring her small ritual.

"You look beautiful," he said.

Pea blushed and looked around the room. The restaurant was crowded, almost every table taken. She hadn't noticed as they had been led to their table.

"Can I order for you, or would that be too old-fashioned?" he asked,

"Please do. I have a feeling that you know exactly what their best meals are," she laughed.

It seemed to her that the evening took on a brighter and more relaxed turn at that point. She began to talk this time, answering his questions, talking about her home, her horses, her parents' deaths, her sister whom she called "Ree", and finally, about her divorce.

She couldn't bring herself to tell him about Alicia, though. It didn't seem the time to open that particular wound for his examination.

Several hours passed as they laughed and talked and enjoyed the food that Trey had very correctly described as delicious. As they talked, he had reached his hand across the table and touched hers gently and she felt as if little shocks were traveling along her wrist bone.

Am I going to do something I'll regret, she wondered. She had thought she wouldn't need anything like this again, but, God, his touch felt so right.

By the time he had taken her to his house, a small 18th century brick building wedged between an alley and another historic house, she knew she had no choice. She needed him right now to take her pain away, if just for one night.

With the exception of the small table lamp next to the front door, they didn't even stop to turn other lights on. They fell against one another, removing their clothes as they almost ran the steps toward his second floor bedroom suite.

By the time they had reached the bed, he was shirtless and she was standing before him in just her underwear, pearls and boots. He sat her down at the end of the bed and removed each boot, slowly caressing the inside of each thigh as he did so.

Without waiting she reached out and grasped his neck, pushing herself down onto him, kissing him hard while unbuttoning and unzipping his pants.

Only the full moon pouring through the windows on each side of the bed illuminated their bodies as they began their discovery of one another. His muscled arms and hard chest felt so right against her softness as they began to make love

It was only when they had finished, that he saw tears glistening upon her cheeks. He kissed her lips and pulled him to her. He mistook the tears for the pain from the divorce and her hurt heart.

"Don't cry. I won't hurt you."

She pushed him away from her slightly.

"It's not that. There are . . . is, something I haven't told you." She wondered how big a mistake she was about to make. Some men would not want to hear how broken she was the first time they were together.

He propped himself up on one elbow and looked down at her. They had forgotten her pearls in their lust and each small pearl was as luminescent as her skin in the moonlight. He touched them and took a deep breath. He was going to let her take her time in telling him whatever her secret was. This was one thing he knew he couldn't ask because she wouldn't say it until she was ready.

Pea's tears began again and she reached up to touch his cheek.

"I had a daughter. Alicia. She was six years old and she died and it was my fault." The story of the first show, the palomino, the whole horrible night poured out of her.

When she stopped talking, he pulled her to him. God, he wanted to ease her pain, but this wasn't a pain that just went away. "It's ok, Pea. I'm here. Just hold on and let it out."

He kissed the top of her head and held her as she wept harder than she had since she had lost Alicia. She felt as if she had let a damn burst within herself where she had kept all that pain blocked and she could feel her shaking body release into him her broken heart.

After her tears began to stop, she lifted her head and began to kiss him again and this time they made love once more, gently and tenderly. She fell asleep in his arms feeling safe for the first time in two years.

# CHAPTER 13

When she woke the next morning, he was gone and she tried to think about how much had transpired last night. Did I screw this up, she wondered. She was starting to rise from the bed to look for her clothing when he appeared at the top of the steps, shirtless and in a pair of faded Levis, carrying two mugs of coffee.

"Cream and lots of sugar. Right?" he asked and smiled as he walked to her and kissed her lightly. She could still feel small sparks of desire between them as they stood close and she took the mug and sat back down against the headboard, making sure to pull the sheet up across her breasts.

He sat his mug down on the table opposite and plopped down on the bed next to her. He pulled the sheet away slightly and made as if to peek under it, grinning. She lightly slapped at his hand, sat her cup down and rolled toward him.

"I've got to drive back home this morning. I have animals waiting," she said. "And as much as I'd like to stay here in your bed, I think you probably have things to do today as well."

He sat up, feigning shock.

"Why Miss Pea, I have nothing planned but to be at your service today."

She giggled and pushed at him. "Stop that or I'll start to believe you and I really do have to go home."

"Then take me with you."

Her eyes widened. Did he really want to spend the day with her?

"Really? It's a long, boring drive and a small farm in the middle of nowhere," she asked.

"Absolutely. I want to see this place you describe as almost perfect. Besides, I want to see you in your natural habitat. I've decided to study peas and you're a perfect specimen to start with."

She burst out laughing and threw her pillow at him as she rose to dress, this time not taking the sheet and pulled on her clothing.

She turned back to him. He was watching her movements closely. "What?"

"Nothing," he said. "Just watching." He picked up his mug and drained it.

"Let me find a shirt and we can go. Well, that is after you tell me where you parked," he laughed.

"Oh, God, I forgot about my car. I bet I've gotten ten tickets." She abruptly stopped talking and thought about her day yesterday before her date with Trey. She decided not to go into that with him. She had unloaded enough on him last night and it was possible that he could develop Mary's attitude and put himself in the middle of the whole thing. And she just didn't want to make this wonderful morning go sour.

He pulled a black t-shirt and socks from a drawer in his bureau and dressed quickly, even getting his sneakers on before she could finish zipping her boots.

"C'mon. Time's wasting and I want to start that pea study."

They laughed as they left his house and walked across town toward her car.

# CHAPTER 14

They arrived at the farm before noon. Pea hoped that Mr. Dickson had fed the dogs as well as the horses. She hated to think of them going hungry.

The minute her Audi came around the corner of the house into the back lawn, the two great danes bounded from the long porch that spanned the rear of the house to the gravel drive. Before Trey could exit the car, Pea leapt from the driver's seat and held a hand up in the air. The two dogs immediately sat and froze in place.

"That's quite a trick," Trey said as he extricated himself from the small passenger seat of the Audi.

"Watch this," she said and took her raised hand and flattened it while still holding her arm up. Both dogs instantly lay down and placed their large heads upon their giant paws.

Trey walked around the car to where Pea stood and stared at the dogs. One of them raised his lip as Trey neared Pea while the other one lowered his head and began to growl.

Pea was a bit perturbed. The dogs had never disobeyed her commands, no matter who the visitor was. That they would do so with Trey was discomfiting. She wanted him to like them. They had been her salvation for the last two years, her only friends and her constant companions. She bought them from a breeder in Charleston as puppies after Manley left and though she had never intended to buy two dogs, she found she couldn't separate the siblings. She also had not clipped their ears. She had no intention of ever showing any animal again, be it horse or dog.

"I hope they're not growling because they're hungry," Trey said, trying to break the tension of the moment. Pea began to laugh and the dogs relaxed a bit.

"C'mon boys. Let's see if Mr. Dickson has some chow for you.

As they walked from the drive to the barn, Trey marveled at how well maintained the farm was. Pea had given him the impression that she had let it decline in the last few years, but the grounds were immaculate, with daffodils blooming bright yellow along the back porch of the house.

"Do you have a lawn service?" he questioned.

She shook her head no.

"Then who does the grounds' work? Your Mr. Dickson?"

Again, Pea shook her head.

"He does some of it, but I do most of it. I have a big John Deere mower and I spend a couple of days a week in warmer weather out here working. I've always loved the gardening part of the farm. It was something my Mom and I did together, although she was so much better with plants than I am."

Trey paused for a moment and looked around. The back lawn alone was almost an acre to the wire cow fence that separated the pastures. It was a lot of ground for one person to cover. No wonder she was so trim and in such good shape. She'd have to be to take care of this place with just one old man to lend a hand.

As they neared the barn he could see black and white Holsteins in the distance. Some of them looked large with unborn calves.

"Those aren't your cattle are they?"

Pea laughed and said no, explaining about the pasture lease arrangement she had with a few cattle farmers.

"Hmm, I was about to think you never slept if you had cattle, horses, and the grounds to take care of," he said as they entered the barn.

She called Mr. Dickson's name and Trey heard an voice respond from the rear of the building. An older man in a pair of old tan work pants, worn blue shirt, and an old baseball cap walked toward them.

"I've taken care of the animals, miss. Fed them both last night and this morning and I was getting ready to let the horses out into the pasture when you arrived."

"Thank you, Mr. Dickson. I'll lead them out there myself. I missed them this morning. Oh, let me introduce you. This is Trey Thornton from Lexington."

Trey stepped forward and shook the older man's calloused hands. He had to be at least 75, Trey thought. How much could he really help Pea here?

"Nice to meet you, Mr. Thornton. Well, then, miss, I'm going to get back to my chores," Dickson said and walked back into the dark of the barn.

After Pea had led the three horses to the pasture, she and Trey went into her home to have a late breakfast. Without speaking much, they worked together, she making a pot of what she called "cowboy coffee" that he found unbelievably strong. He scrambled eggs and fried slices of fresh bacon. She was finishing squeezing fresh orange juice just as he announced the eggs and bacon were ready.

She hadn't felt comfortable in the presence of anyone in this kitchen other than Mary in a long time. As they ate in silence, she watched him and marveled that they had needed very few words between them.

"Now, I get to ask. What?" he asked.

Pea shook her head.

"Nothing," she said as she sipped her coffee. "I guess I'm a little surprised to see you here. It really is boring if you don't like the country."

Now it was his turn to shake his head.

"Ah, but you forgot that I grew up on a farm in Augusta County. Remember?"

Oh, she thought, how had I forgotten that?

"Do you still have it?"

"The farm?" he asked.

Trey nodded yes as he drained the juice from his glass.

"But, I don't get up there very much. I have some people who come once a week and take care of things. Since I've been living in Lexington, I've thought about selling it, but, well, it's been in the family so long and I'm the last of them, so . . ."

Pea understood that completely. The farm was such a part of her that she found it hard to believe that she could ever part with it or leave. Besides,

Alicia was here, next to her parents and grandparents. She remembered hearing someone say once when she was younger that some people could never leave a place where someone they loved was buried. Maybe that was part of it. Maybe she was stuck here and couldn't leave.

"Pea? Pea?"

She looked from the window to Trey and realized she had drifted away for a moment.

"Sorry. I was thinking about what these old farms mean to us. I wonder sometimes why I can't seem to leave and Ree couldn't wait to leave. Was she stronger?"

Trey shook his head and rose to gather his dishes to take to the sink.

"No. I think you had more reasons to stay."

After the breakfast dishes were finished, Pea led him out past the pasture where the horses grazed toward a small area surrounded by a low iron fence. He knew it was the family cemetery before they came close to it. He deeply loathed cemeteries and dropped her hand as they neared it.

She stepped over the low fence and moved to a small marble monument that looked almost new. She stood before the grave and stared at it without turning back toward him. She did not know that he had backed away from the cemetery or that he had found something in a different direction to place his stare.

When she turned back to him she saw that his face was white and drawn. She walked out of the small plot to him and took his hand.

"I'm sorry. We can head back to the house."

He dropped her hand once more as they walked back toward the back lawn and Pea was confused. Yesterday and today had gone so well. She had assumed that he wouldn't mind coming out here to where Alicia was and now she could see how wrong she was. He was so quiet and only the sound of the dogs running forward to them and placing themselves between the two of them broke the unnerving quiet of the moment. And still, he didn't say anything, just moved away from the two big dogs.

Pea watched the great danes and saw that they were alert to his every movement. It was as if they would brook no intruders into Pea's life, especially Trey. She suddenly shooed them away, saying, "Home dogs. Go. Now." They galloped away from her back to the porch where they took their watchful positions again.

As they reached the Audi, Pea finally spoke, unable to continue the strange silence.

"I can drive you back to Lexington now, if you'd like. I suppose you want to get home and, and have things to do other than wander around here with me. Just let me run in the house and grab my purse."

Trey stopped suddenly and grabbed her arm. The dogs both leapt to the bottom of the steps and stopped themselves.

He raised his eyebrows and laughed quietly.

"Damn, those dogs are protective of you. I don't think I have to worry about you being out here alone."

Pea's confusion only grew.

"Well, of course not. Why would you?"

"Pea." He paused, unsure as to how to continue. "You've been hurt pretty bad and I'm not sure . . . I know we've only been around each other a couple days, but . . ."

He shrugged his shoulders and looked down at the ground.

"I thought last night you could see that I care about you, more than just the sex."

Pea blushed and stood back from him.

"I thought you wanted to leave, that I was boring you." She spread her arms out and moved around as if demonstrating what she was saying. "This is my life, Trey. It's not much, but it's all I have." She lifted her chin a bit that same way she had yesterday when Joseph had disapproved of her plans.

Trey moved to her and placed his hands upon her shoulders. He could see the dogs inching forward in the corner of his eye.

"Pea, I don't find you or your life boring. Can't you see that? I want to be here."

She shivered as she heard those words. She had heard the same words come from Manley's mouth. The "I want to be where ever you are" speech. She inched away from him and froze up. Now the dogs were very close and growling.

Trey took a deep breath and looked over at them and as he did Pea noticed them as well. She held up her hand and flattened it and the dogs went down immediately.

Trey blew out a puff of air into the afternoon that was starting to turn chilly.

"I hope I never see the kill signal to them," he said and turned back to her. She was staring out at the pasture at the horses.

"Sorry," he said.

"I heard those words once before," she said.

Shit, her ex. Again. He felt like he was fighting a losing battle here.

"I am not him. I don't see a lot of women. I work for myself and I spend more time by myself than I do with people. I read a lot. I have my own farm and my own money," he stopped a minute to calm down before continuing.

"I don't need anything from you, but I do want to be with you. If you can't believe me, if you can't trust me, maybe I should go." He put his hands in his jacket pockets. It was his turn to look away toward the horses.

Pea returned her gaze to him. What was she thinking? He was right. He was nothing like Manley. What the hell was wrong with her? Mary was right. She had to leave the past and start moving on.

"It's just that you became so quiet. I thought something was wrong and then, and then," she was unable to continue.

"And then I said something that you'd heard before from someone who had betrayed you." He moved back from her.

"I can't change the past, Pea. And I became quiet because I really, really hate cemeteries and I hated what I saw it was doing to you."

She rubbed her hands together to warm them up.

"Do you want me to take you home?"

"Do you want me to go?" he asked in return.

She shook her head. "No. I don't."

"Okay, then can we go inside where it's warm and talk some more." He looked at the dogs who were still watching them closely. "Are they hungry again?" He asked and smiled that crooked smile that she was beginning to truly like.

She laughed and said no, and they walked past the dogs and into the house. The dogs followed and took up their usual spots next to the sofa.

# CHAPTER 15

Trey woke the next morning in Pea's bed. It was an antique iron bed that someone had painted with gold radiator paint a long, long time ago. It was also only a full size bed and he found that they had wrapped themselves around each other in the night as they slept. Before he had lain with her there, he had had to ask her if it had been her bed for long.

"You mean is this the bed I shared with . . . him?"

He hadn't wanted to ask this, but he refused to sleep with ghosts last night, even the ghosts of former relationships.

"No," she replied. "This was always my bed. The only other person who climbed in with me was Ree when we were children. I never slept with anyone else in it. Well, maybe a couple of dogs when they were still puppies."

He had nodded his head and then looked over at the danes lying in the hallway.

"I gave the other bed away and that room is used for storage now. Nothing in this room but me," she had said.

Trey extricated himself from her in the early morning light and almost stepped on one of the dogs as he tried to get up from the bed. The dogs had bookended the bed during the night while they slept, but this morning they were rather unresponsive to him. The one on his side of the bed looked up at him for a moment and then stood and stretched.

Trey tentatively moved his hand out to touch the dog and as he did, the dog moved over to him and laid his head on Trey's knee.

"Guess I passed muster last night with you, big guy," Trey whispered and continued to pet the beast. He stood and grabbed his jeans from the end of the bed and said to the dog, "C'mon. Let's go find some chow." As he dressed he looked out at the pasture toward the thick spring fog that rolled in most mornings in the valley. He could see why Pea loved it here so much. It was a very different farm from his family's and there was a peace that seemed to emanate from the land itself.

He shook his head as he thought about what a selfish bastard her ex had been.

He glanced down at Pea sleeping in the bed, her arm stretched out to where he had been. She looked so calm when she slept, as if all her worries disappeared in her dreamland.

He went downstairs and stuck a cup of last night's coffee in the microwave to reheat and then opened the kitchen doors to walk out onto the back porch. The danes immediately rushed past him and headed out to the barn. He sat down on the porch steps and watched them gallop away. Obviously they knew where they needed to be this morning and he was a bit relieved that they no longer seemed to see him as an intruder.

Pea and her animals seemed to have a unique relationship in his mind and he didn't want to be the one on the losing end if he couldn't get along with the dogs. He had never seen any animals so fiercely loyal to anyone before. He supposed they had seen many more of her tears than he had and as he sipped the bitter coffee, he was glad she had had them then.

It was much cooler this morning and the dampness of the fog was different from the more humid spring mornings of the Shenandoah Valley. It reminded him of home, but it wasn't like Augusta County where the land was more crowded now and much less quiet.

He walked back into the house and headed back upstairs to Pea's bedroom. They had talked long into the evening before going upstairs and he felt as if he understood something more of what she had gone through in the past decade than he had before. And he had found himself opening up to her as well, talking about his loneliness growing up after his mother had died and his father had retreated into himself.

Trey's father had never accepted his mother's death and he believed that his father had literally mourned himself to death, dying too soon and too young and yet looking too old for his age. He told Pea that there was a similar family plot on his family farm like the one on hers where her daughter now was. He told her that he had at first been very angry with his father for giving up and he had refused to go to the plot to visit either of their graves. And now, he had said, I just don't want to be around cemeteries. Maybe because of guilt. He told her he really couldn't explain it.

She was still sleeping when he walked back into the bedroom and he undressed and got back into bed with her, bringing her body closer, letting it warm the chill from his skin.

She opened her eyes and smiled lightly, reaching her arms around his back.

"You're cold. Where have you been?"

"Drinking your weird coffee on the back porch."

She laughed. "It's not weird. It's just an old-fashioned way of making coffee."

He tipped her face up to his and kissed her, brushing her pale blonde hair away from her face.

"You know, there's been this great new invention called a coffeemaker. You can even set it up to have the coffee brewed and waiting for you when you get up."

He kissed her forehead and continued.

"Actually, there have been quite a few inventions in the last 50 years that have made cooking easier."

She groaned as she rolled onto her back and gazed at the ceiling where she had placed glow-in-the-dark stars and comets when she had been little. They were still there, the one part of her childhood she had left intact.

"Ugh, cooking. I have to tell you another secret. I'm a lousy cook. It bores me to tears. There are so many other things I'd rather do than that. What's so funny is that Ree, the great, ambitious soon-to-be lawyer, is a fabulous cook. I guess I missed that gene in the genetic lottery"

"I think you got other talents instead, but you have to eat something, especially out here," he said.

"I have simple tastes. A steak and a baked potato. A hamburger. A salad. Those are easy. I can cook those and I can buy them once a week without having to drive into Lewisburg every day," she said and turned back to him.

"You know I have to go back today."

She sighed and nodded her assent.

"But we don't have to leave immediately." He pulled her closer and began to make love to her, this time without any sadness or tears or unsaid words left between them.

"Oh, that's a good idea, waiting to leave."

# CHAPTER 16

While the next month was spent mostly with Trey, Pea also continued her quest for Pearl, keeping the knowledge of it away from both Mary and Trey.

Too often she felt as if they treated her as one of Alicia's fragile china dolls and she wasn't. It seemed that only Joseph and Thomas Washington had come to believe that she wasn't.

And that meeting had been a bigger matter than she had expected. The two men were bristly with one another, neither quite trusting each other, but agreeing to work together because of Pea and her insistence that they could figure this out. And what had they discovered so far?

Joseph had "self requisitioned" an empty office near his and had bribed the janitor for a key and his silence. There the three of them had worked when they could get away, charting the mysteries of the women's disappearances and murders over the past twelve years.

Joseph had taken one blank wall and had used it to place the photos of the women upon it, with the last known dates they had been seen, and in some cases, the dates that their bodies had been found.

That night was the first time Thomas had seen it and it had upset him immensely when he saw the wall and saw Shawnette's picture there. His hands became fists and for a moment she thought he might hit either Joseph or the wall. But he hadn't. After the initial shock, he sat down and just stared at the photos of the twelve women. It was incomprehensible to him that someone could murder these beautiful young women, much less why.

Joseph had patiently tried to explain the pathology behind it, but Thomas was still too bereft to fully acknowledge what was on that wall and so Joseph and Pea both had waited in patient silence until he was ready to accept it.

"Who are we looking for?" he finally asked.

Joseph came round the table holding Shawnette's red journal in his hand.

"We know more than we would have because of what Shawnette wrote. She gave us some clues to who was following her, a good description of the car, but not a good description of what the man looked like. But we do know we're looking for a man who's probably in his mid-thirties by now, possibly white or Hispanic or even a light skinned African-American."

Pea looked at the wall.

"Why these women?" She asked. "Other than race, sex and age, they have almost nothing in common. They don't look alike. They come from different parts of the two counties and, for the most part, very different lives, well, with the exception of the ones who were prostitutes."

Joseph joined her at the wall, putting both his hands in his pockets and studying the information there.

"That's a very good question. Ok, first victim Pearl Marie Montgomery, 20. Disappeared June 1, 1998. Body never found.

"Second victim Mattie Sue White, 25, prostitute. Last seen June 7, 1999 at the Waynesboro Truck Stop. Body not recovered.

"Third victim Winnie Jean Thompson, 21, Drug addict. Last seen June 18, 2000, Waynesboro, Virginia. Body not recovered."

He paused and then moved on.

"Fourth. Pharah Marie Knight, 27, prostitute who disappeared in Staunton on May 30, 2001. And again, body not recovered.

"Fifth to go was Teresa Jane Ledbetter, 24, waitress at the truck stop in Waynesboro, Virginia. Disappeared June 3, 2003 from the parking lot. Her car was found there, but her body was not found.

"Sixth victim was Deelee King, 24, Staunton prostitute who disappeared June 15, 2004. Now we have the first real evidence of murder. Her body was discovered in November 2007 by a hunter in Goshen, Virginia, along with the bodies of Karen Marie Martin and Margret Ellis."

Joseph turned back to Pea and Thomas.

"How the hell did the police not see this? Even the Green River Killer started making people suspicious after the fourth woman disappeared." He shook his and turned back to the wall.

"Number Seven. Karen Marie Martin, 33, resident of Staunton. No drug or prostitution history. No arrest record. Last seen leaving her house on June 14, 2005. She was murdered. And, as I said of Deelee King, her body discovered in November 2007 with the bodies of Deelee and Margret Ellis.

"Eighth victim. Margaret Ellis, 28, of Waynesboro. She, too, had a history of drug use. She disappeared May 28, 2006. Murdered. Her body discovered with the bodies of Deelee King and Karen Marie Martin.

"Nine. Nina Ruth Smith, 18, Staunton resident who disappeared June 2, 2007. Again, murdered. Her body recovered from the Jackson River July 4, 2008.

"Ten. Alicia Mary Trent, 27, single mother of two girls and a waitress." He stopped again. "Now she is the only victim who wasn't from either Staunton or Waynesboro. She disappeared June 17, 2008 from Lexington. She, too, was murdered and her body was dumped along the Jackson River, but wasn't found until 2009."

Joseph looked to Thomas. He dreaded this.

"Shawnette. Shawnette Davis, 20, student at Mary Baldwin College, Last seen at Valu-Mart in Staunton, Virginia, May 27, 2009. Shawnette's body was found along the Jackson River near the remains of Alicia Trent."

"And last, found almost exactly where Shawnette was found was Sharon Ann Barger, 28, a prostitute from Staunton who disappeared June 17, 2009. And her body was found July 30, 2009."

Pea pointed at the wall.

"He accelerated last year. Two women in less than two months. Why?" she asked.

"We're missing something here." Joseph sighed deeply, and faced Thomas, who had remained silent throughout his recitation.

"Look, we're all tired and if I don't get home to Mary, she's going to come looking for me and you," he directed at Pea, "do not want that."

She agreed. She was supposed to be at Trey's in a half hour and she disliked lying to him about any of this. Thomas stood and walked to the door.

"I need a longer break than just this evening. This is more than I had expected to get involved in. Can we talk next week? I really don't want to do this now," he said and walked out the door and away from them.

Pea felt so bad for him. He was the one who had really lost someone. This wasn't just a mystery to him. It was his life. Both she and Joseph should have been more cognizant of that.

"Joseph, let's step back for a bit and maybe come back with fresh eyes. I don't think either one of us is doing well hiding this from Ree or Trey."

Joseph nodded his agreement and they walked out of his office building together, deciding that they would call Thomas later in the week and try to start again.

Joseph watched Pea as she walked down the street toward Trey's house. Neither he nor Mary had met Trey yet and that bothered him a little bit. Actually it bothered Mary a whole lot. She was very overprotective of her sister and had it not been for the last weeks of school coming up, she would have been on Trey's doorstep looking for Pea.

As Pea disappeared, he began to walk in the opposite direction towards Mary's apartment. She would graduate in a few weeks and his guest lectureship would be over. He brooded a bit over that. He did not like not knowing where they would be in such a short time. He liked plans. Solid plans. And there was nothing solid about this plan. There wasn't even a plan or a promise other than the one he had made to her that night. Now he wondered if she had just wanted him to say it because she was afraid of whatever future might be barreling toward them.

As he neared her apartment, he stopped and looked up to see her in the window studying. How could he leave her? It was just too hard to even think about, he thought, and he entered the building where she waited for him.

# CHAPTER 17

Trey had just finished cooking dinner for Pea and was starting to think she had disappeared on him when he heard her in the front hall. How long did she and her sister talk? Sometimes it seemed as if she spent more time there than here. And then he thought that wasn't a fair thing to think since they had only been together for a month or so. Ree was her rock, he supposed.

"I stopped for wine," she said as she walked into his kitchen. "Didn't know whether to get red or white, so I got white."

He laughed as he took the bottle from her and began to remove the cork.

"White is fine since we're having broiled salmon and steamed saffron rice."

"Wow. Well, at least I found someone to feed me," she said and kissed him.

"So that's why you keep coming back."

She removed her coat and walked up behind him and hugged his back.

"Oh, I can think of a few other reasons to keep coming back."

He turned back around so that her arms encircled his waist and kissed her full mouth.

"As much as I'd like to keep doing this, I'm also very hungry. What on earth do you and your sister talk about for so long?"

Pea blushed in shame. She had lied about being at Mary's and Joseph had lied to Mary about grading tests. Neither of them could keep this up much longer. She knew that if Mary and Trey discovered what they and Thomas Washington had been really doing that they would be furious. The thought that Trey might not want to see her again flashed in her head for a brief second and terrified her. She was going to have to find the courage to tell him the truth. Soon. And she prayed he would forgive her deception.

"We talk about school and family stuff. Boring girl stuff. I'm starved," she said, quickly changing the subject, but she saw his shoulders stiffen slightly. He was feeling excluded. He had asked her about meeting Mary and she had hesitated, saying that between Mary's complex dating situation and her upcoming finals and bar exam, she didn't have much time to socialize.

"Yeah, family stuff. Ok," he said and removed the salmon from the oven and placed it on the table.

"Trey. I didn't mean it that way. I was talking about the farm and all the legal stuff with it."

He sat down across from her and poured the wine into the two Waterford goblets.

"It's ok. I do understand. I just expected you earlier."

She started to apologize again, but stopped herself. She had to tell him. Soon.

"I need to go home this weekend, Trey. I've really been away a lot and I need to check on the house and the dogs. Go with me?" she asked.

"Can't," he said. "I need to go up to Staunton and check on my place up there. Make sure the roof's not falling in. I haven't been up there in months and even though the caretaker keeps me up to date on things, I still need to check it out for myself."

He didn't look up at her, but began eating, so he wouldn't have to explain further. He could sense her frustration, but he was a little pissed off at her and he knew he shouldn't be cold to her, but still he was frustrated as well.

"Oh, well, I guess you need to go alone," she said.

He finally raised his head from his plate.

"Do you want to go with me? I could show you where I grew up, unless you absolutely have to go back home this weekend. We could drive up tomorrow afternoon. If you want, that is."

Pea smiled and drank her wine in one drink.

"That sounds great. I can find out all your deep dark secrets up there," she said.

He laughed. "Not too many dark secrets up there. Just my dad's old Buick and some ugly Victorian furniture my great-grandmother collected.

"Oh, everybody has dark secrets. It's what makes them so, so sexy," she said as she rubbed her stockinged foot against the inside of his leg.

"You are absolutely determined that I don't get to eat."

"Hmm. I am hungry, but I could always think of other things to do than eat," she said.

"I bet you could, but Miss Pea, I'm going to eat this meal that I cooked for you first. So take that pretty little foot and put it back in your slipper."

She sniffed, acting slightly offended.

"If you hadn't noticed, I've finished my meal."

She held up her empty plate.

"Look. My plate is clean, so," she continued as she rose from the table. "I'm going on upstairs and maybe crawl in that giant claw foot tub you have."

She lowered her eyes a bit. "And if you ever finish eating, you could bring that bottle and meet me upstairs."

He watched as she walked toward the stairs with her goblet in hand.

Damn, he thought and ate his meal quickly, was on his feet and following her with the bottle of wine and his own goblet before he knew it.

By the time he had reached the bathroom, she was already deep in bubbles, reclining with her eyes closed in the soft light of the candles she had lit around the tub.

After he had undressed and climbed in the other end, she didn't open her eyes. Shit, he thought, she's asleep, just as she opened one eye and peeked at him.

"Don't do that or I leave you here like a drowned cat," he said.

She moved through the water and bubbles toward him and kissed him and laughed

"Oh, you don't want to do that when we can find some other things to do instead."

By 9 a.m. the next morning, they were driving up I-81 to Staunton in Trey's Celica, Lady Antebellum playing in the background.

Pea waved her hand in rhythm to the music. As they passed the Waynesboro exit, she thought about the women who had gone missing from the truck stop there, one a prostitute and the other a single mother working a double-shift as a waitress. Pea, as hard as it was losing a child, could not imagine the pain that the small child of that waitress was feeling as the three year old girl waited for her mother to return.

Pea's hand dropped to her lap and she felt an immense sadness for those women and their families. So much pain. So much pain.

But Trey had not noticed the sudden shift in her mood and had reached over to squeeze her hand.

"You have the oddest tastes in music. Is there anything you don't like? One minute I'm listening to Cee Lo Green and the next minute Steve Martin playing Bluegrass. I think your music gene is schizoid," he said and laughed.

She squeezed his hand back and smiled.

"I just like good music. It takes me places, especially playing."

"Then why haven't you ever played for me?"

She took a deep breath.

"You don't have a piano."

'No, I don't. But you do and you've never played when I've been at your house," he said.

Pea squirmed a bit in the seat. How to tell him this? Why was getting to know someone such a difficult process sometimes? Or maybe, she thought, letting someone get to know me?

"I used to play all the time when people were around and even when I was alone. I could play for hours and not think about anything. Just feel the music. But,"

Another deep breath.

"I was told that my playing was mediocre and bored friends, so I stopped playing for anyone but myself. I was embarrassed. But I still play a lot when I'm alone. When I'm home, I often play an hour or more every day."

Trey looked over at her and shook his head. Getting angry with her ghosts only made her defensive. That was one thing he had discovered about her in the past few months.

As they took the Staunton exit and headed north on 11 toward Fort Defiance, they were both quiet. As they drove the route, she wondered where Pearl had been on this road almost 12 years ago, but Trey was still obsessing with the music.

"Well, I've a surprise. I do have a piano at the farm. I have no idea what kind of condition it's in, but you can check it out for me while I go through some paperwork with the caretakers."

Pea sat up straighter and began to tense up. Pearl slipped from her mind and all she could imagine was his hearing her play poorly.

"I'm not that good. I don't think I could tell you much."

"You've played since you were five. I'm sure you know at least something about pianos."

As they passed the old Augusta Military Academy and the Old Stone Church, they neared a secondary road that led off into a small valley road on which they continued for more than a few miles.

"I think you live as far away from town as I do in Greenbrier," she said as the rolling scenery passed by.

"Pretty much," he said as he pulled onto a dirt road. In the distance she could see a large brick antebellum Virginia farmhouse that made her family farmhouse look small in comparison.

"Wow." She whistled as she exited the Celica and looked up at the house. She walked around the car to Trey's side and stared at the formidable two story building.

"It's huge. How much of the land is yours?"

"All of it. 2,500 acres. The full original land grant plus acreage that came as dowries from my different grandmothers' families. More than I need. Come on. Let's go on in."

As they ascended the white stone steps, she looked out toward the different sections of the land. Very few fences and the barn looked unused for decades.

Inside the house, she found he had been right. The furniture was a hideous mish-mash of mid 20th century pieces and late Victorian extravagance. She guessed that his mother had never really had a chance to change anything.

In the front parlor, she saw the old upright piano in the far corner of the room and she relaxed a bit. The thing probably had broken strings and rotted felts and hammers. Little luck of it actually being something she would have to play.

"I'll get our bags a little later. I called the Franklins and asked them to stock the fridge and open the house up so we should be able to make it through a few days here," he said.

"But I'm going to let you look at the piano. I've got to go outside and find Mr. Franklin and check on some other things."

"Sure," she said and smiled brightly. "I'll be fine. Go ahead and I'll explore."

"Well, if you find gold or a lost treasure map, let me know. I think I hid them here somewhere when I was a kid."

He kissed her lightly on the cheek and headed out the front door.

She decided to get the piano question over first and she sat down on an old fashioned round stool and lifted the lid off the keys. Story and Clark. She could have predicted that. A good brand, but one that she often had found in the past in poor condition. On the top of the piano she found some music sheets, mostly classical and mostly Mozart and Beethoven. She found the Moonlight Sonata and placed it on the music holder before her. Here goes nothing, she thought and laughed.

She could not have been more surprised when the key action and tone was perfect. She stopped for second. This piano should not play this well. She turned toward the door and realized Trey had had the piano tuned recently and probably for her. Sneaky son of a bitch, she thought, but she nevertheless turned back to the piano and began to play.

Outside on the portico, Trey waited to hear the first notes. When she suddenly stopped and then a few seconds later began to play the sonata perfectly, he laughed and walked over toward to the garage to find Mr. Franklin. He had called up earlier in the week, hoping that she'd come with him this weekend and making arrangements for the piano to be taken care of and the other things necessary for the weekend.

"Now, that sounds wonderful. A sound I haven't heard from that house in many years. Good to see you Charles," Franklin said as Trey walked to him."

Trey turned back to look at the house. Even at this distance, he could hear the music pouring out the open window. It was a wonderful thing to hear.

The piano had been his mother's and one of his favorite memories from his childhood was of playing on the carpet with his Matchbox Cars while she played Beethoven and Mozart effortlessly. It was his best memory of his mother before she died. He liked to think that she would have liked Pea.

"Everything's been taken care of that you asked for when you called on Monday," Franklin said. "The only problem I'm having is with your dad's Buick. I think it needs a new alternator. I'll have to go to NAPA to see if they can get one for me. It might be hard for a car this old."

"Do what you can and we'll go from there," Trey replied. "What about the barn? Have you had anyone out to check it for damage to the support beams?"

Franklin nodded. "Yeah, it's in much better shape than it looks. Nothing that a fresh coat of paint won't cure."

"Ok, then let's do that. I'd like to come up more often and I'd like to get the place back into good shape."

Franklin smiled. "I'm glad to hear that, Charles. Your family would be happy to think of you being here again."

Trey started to walk back to the house. "Do you have the money you need in the account to get the repairs done?"

"If I don't, I'll give you a call in Lexington. By the way, do you want the missus to cook for you this weekend?"

"No," Trey said. "I think you both can take the rest of the weekend off. No need to stay up here this weekend. Go see your grandkids. I'd say Margaret won't argue with that," and he smiled as he left Franklin closing the door to the garage.

The music had stopped by the time he reentered his home and looked in the parlor for Pea. Exploring. She was somewhere in the house. He stood still for a minute and then heard her out toward the kitchen and went in that direction.

# CHAPTER 18

He found her in the tiny kitchen looking in the fridge.

"Hungry?"

She jumped at the sound of his voice and closed the refrigerator door quickly.

"I was looking for a Coke or a soft drink. I wanted a caffeine fix and," she extended her arms around the kitchen, "I have no idea where a coffee pot or coffee might be in here."

He walked over to an old Hoosier cabinet and pulled a glass jar from it labeled Coffee. He then went to one of the cabinets above the farm sink and pulled down a coffee pot.

"I just have one request. Use the strainer. No cowboy coffee. Please?"

"Well, then you make it. It's your house, after all," she sat down at the tiny enamel top table.

"Did you get some of your business taken care of?" she asked.

He finished getting the coffee on the old stove and moved to sit down opposite her at the table.

"Yes, well not everything, but some things are going to have to be done later."

"Such as?"

"My dad's old car. I've got to either fix it or get rid of it. I should just sell it. And I need to get the barn painted. I had it inspected and it's in good shape except for the paint.

She looked around the kitchen.

"What about the house? Is it as sound as the piano?"

He dipped his head down and tried to suppress a smile.

"Sorry. I wanted to surprise you, but I wasn't sure the tuner had been able to make the repairs in time."

She took his hand and stared at him.

"Thank you. I felt good playing it. You didn't mind?"

"Mind?" he asked, rising to pour the coffee into two brown mugs. "You are not a mediocre musician. You play beautifully. Pea, you've got the kill that voice he put in your head. You're better than he ever let you know. And,"

He sat back down and placed the mugs on the table. "And I'm starting to get tired of hearing his voice in your head." He looked at the table and moved the mug from one hand to the other, waiting to see how she would react.

"You're right. But it was a long time and I'm trying hard not to upset you."

"No, Pea, you're misunderstanding me. I don't want you to do it for me. Do it to remove the bastard from your life. You can't spend the rest of your life under an invisible thumb. You've got to get past it all."

She sipped her coffee and nodded assent. If only he knew how hard it was to do what he was asking of her, she thought. If only I could forget the cruelty and the shame, she thought. But there's always Alicia falling backward. How was she supposed to forget that? Her stupidity had killed her own child.

She was trying not to cry and so she stood and walked to the kitchen door.

"Mind if I walk around a bit?"

He sighed. "No, go ahead, but stay close to the buildings. There are some groundhog holes in the pasture and you could trip and break a leg."

She was letting one thought after another flow through her mind as she walked around outside. When she came to the garage, she opened the side door and looked for a light switch. Over to one side she saw a string cord hanging from the ceiling. The light filled the garage and she saw the shape of the Buick under a large tarp. She lifted the rear corner and saw that it was in pretty poor shape. It looked like a late 1970s model with what had once been factory green paint and bright chrome bumpers that were now riddled with rust and dull with age and neglect. The car reminded her of the Buick that had trailed Shawnette. But, she thought, it certainly wasn't this Buick. This car hadn't been moved in ages.

She left the garage and was about to walk down to the barn and then stopped to look back at the house. The man she was falling in love with was in there waiting patiently for her to stop feeling sorry for herself and grow up. She would be thirty-two in almost a month. Wasn't it time she stopped being afraid of loving someone, she wondered. Would she get another chance again? She started to walk briskly back to the house.

He was waiting for her and she was ready for him. If she could be the person who was fearlessly looking for Pearl and Shawnette's killer, then she could be the woman who could open up to the man sitting in that kitchen.

If it hurts, if he didn't love her, she could at least tell herself that she had tried.

So, when she swung open the back door and walked into the kitchen to him, he stood quickly and took her in his arms and kissed her hard, holding her as if he let go too lightly she might evaporate. He saw that she had made her decision and he buried his face in her neck.

"I need to say something and if you can't hear it, tell me," she said.

"I just know if I don't say it now, I may never be brave or strong enough to say it."

He didn't want to look at her face. He was too afraid of what she might be about to say. He looked down and saw no signs of tears there, but instead a small tentative frown that formed between her brows.

"Go ahead. You know you can tell me anything. I might be deaf to everyday stuff, but I will always listen to you when you have something important to say," he said.

She looked down for a moment and then up into his dark brown eyes. Here goes nothing, she thought.

"I love you. I think I have since you led me from Winter's that day that I was having a panic attack. It was as if you rescued me and no one had ever done that for me. I was so amazed by you that I couldn't believe you were real. But I didn't realize until I was just outside now and you were sitting in here that I was a fool, that I loved you even if you didn't feel the same." It all poured out of her in one breathless rush.

He was still watching her face when he realized that he had been holding his breath, afraid that she was going to say that she couldn't do this, that she couldn't be with him. Relief flooded his body and he smiled at her.

"I love you, Pea. And I've been waiting a long time to find you. If I'd only known you were just across the state line, I'd have come there to find you."

She buried her face in his chest and held him as tightly as he was holding her. What a change, she thought. How can life change so quickly?

Later she decided to go on her exploration of his home as he went to bring in their bags from the Celica.

"So, I can look anywhere? No Grace Poole on the third floor?" she had asked.

As he was going out the front door, he stopped.

"Grace Poole? Who the hell is Grace Poole?"

She laughed out loud. "You were never an adolescent girl who read the Brontë sisters. Grace Poole hid Mr. Rochester's insane wife on the third floor of his home in *Jane Eyre*."

He shook his head. "No, and if you didn't notice, there is no third floor and I have no wives past or present. Go ahead. Explore the whole place. No Grace Pooles with matches."

"Aha! You have read it."

"I have an excellent education. But I also have a fondness for Masterpiece Theater. So go on now. I have things to tote," he said and waved her on her way as he went to retrieve luggage.

Pea wondered up the center hall staircase and stopped at the center landing where she could get a full view of the foyer. The house must have been magnificent in its heyday. She could imagine Trey's grandmothers in their rustling silks and men in white ties with beaver top hats.

On reaching the second floor, she saw that the hall extended in two long directions. She chose to go right and opened the first door and laughed. A broom closet with cleaning supplies. So much for a secret passage, she thought.

The other rooms in that wing were four bedrooms, one larger room that looked as if it had been used as a nursery of sorts with a tiny bedroom in what looked like a closet, and one very small bath. That must have been the children's wing of the house or rooms for guests who weren't expected to stay very long.

The wing to the left was quite different, fewer rooms, and larger bathrooms. The largest of the rooms seemed to be a small parlor and bedroom suite with a door to an adjoining room that was a bit more masculine with an attached bath. The other three rooms in that section were larger as well, but single bedrooms, each with their own bathrooms.

All of the rooms in the upstairs, as well as the hallway itself, was cluttered with antique and some modern furniture, from all sorts of bedroom furniture to thread winders, spinning wheels, and a 1970s Kenmore sewing machine in a very angular maple cabinet.

She guessed that the furniture in the rooms was as full of old ephemera and old clothing as the rooms were full of furniture. Definitely, generations of one family had lived here, she thought, some probably at the same time which may have made it difficult to dispose of things.

Downstairs, she found smaller rooms off of the large dining room and front parlor – a small study, a linen press, and a few very small bedrooms and two bathrooms that were probably meant for servants many years ago.

But the room she found that she loved the most was the large conservatory at the rear of the house. It was filled with antique paper wicker chairs, tables and empty flower pots of all shapes and sizes everywhere.

Obviously added sometime at the turn of the century, the room had three walls and a partial ceiling almost completely composed of glass windows, with the remaining brick wall dominated by an enormous ceramic tile stove. As with much of the rest of the house, she could see that this room hadn't been used in decades except for storage.

She was examining a long wicker settee when Trey finally located her.

"No Grace Poole, I assume?" he asked.

"No, but what an incredible house! But, I can also see why you don't stay out here much. It's a lot of house for one person."

He looked around the conservatory and up at the high windows. He hadn't spent much time in the room since his mother's death. She wouldn't have been happy with the way it looked now, he thought.

Pea watched him and thought that he must have been lonely here after his mother's death and his father's retreat into grief. She supposed the house evoked a mixture of emotions and memories within him. And then being sent off to boarding school at 12 had probably only made it worse.

She walked over to him and wrapped one arm around his waist. She wasn't quite sure what to say to him now and allowed his silence to continue a bit.

"Well, did you find the large suite? I thought we'd sleep there tonight. It's where I usually stay when I drive up. That ok with you?" he asked.

"That's fine. I loved that first room. Very warm and comfortable," she said. "But I never really saw a room that looked like it had belonged to you. No little boy room with cowboys or spacemen."

He raised his eyebrows in a semi shrug.

"No, no cowboys or spacemen. Mother never had time to really do anything with the house except for this room and now, well, it's just storage, too."

"Come. Let's go put some supper together. I'm getting hungry. Unfortunately, the kitchen is one of the smallest rooms in the house. But, we have food, so we won't go hungry," he said and led her from the conservatory as the sun was starting to move toward the horizon through the windows.

# CHAPTER 19

Joseph Hallett had found that sitting in the apartment with Mary's law books everywhere had started to drive him crazy. She had dry erase boards set up everywhere, the books open on what seemed like every surface, and index cards even taped to door facings.

When he told her he was going over to his office, she nodded absentmindedly and said, "See you later," without even looking up from the book she was studying.

He hoped her inattention to his absence was merely a temporary thing and not an omen of their last weeks together at Washington and Lee. As he walked across the campus to his office, he wondered if he would follow her or if she would even want him to go with her when she was hired as a junior associate somewhere. If it turned out to be near D.C., then his place in Fairfax might serve as a convenience for them both. But, if she chose somewhere else, he might get left behind.

He believed her when she told him she loved him, but Mary had a short attention span when it came to anything outside her wheelhouse of the legal world and he believed he could be loved and left by her at the same time.

The thought of that depressed him a great deal. Not just because Mary would leave, but because he was getting to a point in his life where he had realized that so many opportunities would soon be out of reach. He could go back to the Bureau for a while he supposed or even do consulting for law firms or law enforcement, but he wanted someone to share his life with him as well and he wouldn't mind a family, either. Somewhere along the way, while he was living his life, that part had gotten pushed to the back.

Instead of going to his office, he decided to go to the room he was using with Pea and Thomas to profile the murders of the twelve women. It seemed the only thing he could concentrate on anymore other than the constant tugging at his mind that he might be about to lose Mary and his last chance at any semblance of real happiness in a long term relationship.

As he walked around the table in the second office, looking up at the wall, he came to where Shawnette's red journal lay on the table. He picked it up and leafed back to the last entries she had made. She had noticed an old green Buick several times in the weeks preceding her disappearance. She hadn't been able to see the driver clearly as he had always been parked more than a block away from her every time.

At first she had thought it just a coincidence, but after three weeks of seeing the Buick almost every time she was on the street, she had become afraid.

She wrote that one sunny day with the street full of people that she had decided to go towards the car, instead of walking away from it. Before she was within a half block of it, the car had crossed traffic and into an alley. She said that she had run forward to try to get a glimpse of the license plate, but had only caught the number 8NH in the center of the Virginia tag. Not enough to go to the police with, she had noted.

She also wrote that she had not told Thomas, and she had written a great deal about Thomas – his love, generosity, and strength.

Joseph stopped reading and looked up at the picture of Shawnette that Thomas had brought in, a casual photograph of a beautiful face slightly leaning down, but looking directly into the camera with large bright eyes and smile that must have lit up every room into which she walked.

He understood why Thomas had kept the journal from the police. First, he probably would never have seen it again. It would have disappeared into some cold case box somewhere and it would have been like having her love letters ripped from his hands because Shawnette had clearly trusted and loved Thomas implicitly.

Secondly, the few mentions of their occasional domestic disagreements and his tendency to be overly protective could have been twisted by a prosecutor to shape Thomas as a manically jealous and violent man, though Shawnette had never written of one single instance of violence of any sort by Thomas.

So where did Shawnette's diary leave them?

An older model green Buick in poor shape, a white, Hispanic or light-skinned black male, and the probability that she and the other eleven women had been stalked for at least two weeks before their abduction.

But then there was also the point that had probably kept law enforcement from making a connection – most of the women had been drug addicts, prostitutes, or both, and that the murders had occurred over a very large geographic area. Serial killers tended to range within a specific, small area.

Joseph went back to the wall. In the far corner, he had taped a map of Virginia and West Virginia and had placed yellow push pins for the last sites the women had been seen and red push pins for where bodies had been found.

He went back to the table and opened his briefcase to pull out a spool of thread he had surreptiously taken from the drawer of Mary's night table.

He went to the map and then began to tie small lengths from where one woman had disappeared to where her body had later been found. There was a sad dearth of red pins on the board that necessitated his using only six pieces of string.

One string led from the Waynesboro truck stop, but next to it stood a lone yellow pin representing the disappearance of a prostitute there. There was no corresponding red pin for her or for whom he believed to be the first victim, Pearl Montgomery, whose pin was sitting in Staunton without any precise location as no one could remember seeing her again after she walked away from her mother's apartment.

After looking at the strings and pins for several minutes, he saw that the victims had all been found in two places, either the Jackson River or the Goshen, Virginia area. Then he saw that all the yellow pins were clustered either along Rt. 11 near Staunton, with only two at the Waynesboro Truck

Stop, one near Shawnette Davis's apartment near Mary Baldwin in Staunton and one in Lexington.

"Ah," he said aloud. The killer was hunting in two specific areas and was disposing of bodies in two distinct areas. While Staunton and Waynesboro were very close, the disposal sites had been spaced much further apart. Both the Jackson River and Goshen sites were on the western side of Lexington.

Why so far apart from the abduction sites, he wondered.

What would draw the killer west of Lexington when there were certainly plenty of remote areas in Augusta County to toss out the bodies?

As he pondered these questions, he sat in a folding chair and once more looked at the wall. His eyes were starting to tire and he felt he was still missing something. Maybe Thomas and Pea could bring fresh eyes to this next week.

He took a deep breath, leaned back in the metal chair and began to rub his eyes. He thought about telling Mary tonight, but with her finals next week he knew the timing was absolutely impossible. He did not think that Pea had told her friend, yet. What was his name? Trey. Yes. He didn't think she had told Trey yet.

These southern nicknames confounded him at times. He had never been called anything but Joseph by his very WASPy parents. An attempt, he supposed, by his mother to assimilate herself and to remove any ethnicity from his actual mixed Italian/American heritage, even going so far as anglicizing his middle name from her maiden name of Giordano to Jordan. Instead of being Joseph Giordano Hallett, he was given the name Joseph Jordan Hallett.

He grew up the son of a surgeon whose family had been some of the original settlers of Long Island and an third generation Italian Catholic mother who met his father at New York Presbyterian while doing her doctorate in medical research. Since science had been their only devotion, religion or the lack thereof, had not been a problem for them.

But for his Italian grandmother it had been a horrendous problem. Whenever he went to visit his grandparents, his Nana Giordano had whisked him off to Mass. He knew that there had been stormy arguments about catechism and Catholic school, but the Hallett family had always gone to private school and so in the end Nana Giordano had lost.

He thought of Nana Giordano. She never understood why he chose to be a "police officer" as she called him rather than a lawyer or professor. That was one point on which both sides of his family had agreed. They were baffled by his choice of the FBI after law school, rather than what his father called a "higher calling" into the law and politics.

Joseph knew that they had never and would never understand that he did what he was good at and what he liked just as his parents had. He chuckled for a moment and wondered what their reaction to Mary would be if he were to take her to meet them.

Nana Giordano would be thrilled. She lamented his failure to marry and procreate every time he spoke with her. But his parents? They were so, well, so much a part of Manhattan that a place like Lexington, Virginia was just not something they would understand, much less a woman from a horse farm in West Virginia.

Either way, it probably didn't matter. The situation would probably never be faced. He stood and began to gather his things together to walk back home. He pulled his pants a bit and laughed. One thing he could say that Mary had done for him was make him walk off 10 pounds in the last six months.

As he switched off the lights, he thought of Nana Giordano again. No matter what the next month held for Mary and him, he was going home to Long Island after he finished up here and see Nana Giordano. He missed her and her kitchen that always smelled of home made tomato sauce. It smelled of home.

When he arrived at the apartment, Mary was still sitting cross-legged on the sofa, as if she had not moved from that spot in the last two hours. But he knew better. The smell of tomato sauce wafted from the kitchen. He sat his bag on the chair next to the door and she put her book on the table and jumped up to kiss him.

"I've ignored you. So I made your Nana's sauce and was waiting for you to put on the fettuccine."

"Thank you," he said and kissed her forehead. "Exactly what I need tonight." He began to whistle under his breath as he followed her into the kitchen.

# CHAPTER 20

*May 2009*

Shawnette Davis was running late and in her rush failed to see the Buick parked across the aisle from her car. She had come out of Valu-Mart with her arms loaded with a bag of groceries and her purse as she tried to dig her keys out of her pocket.

Thomas would be home in an hour and she wanted to fix his favorite red snapper. She had introduced him to it on a trip home to Maryland and he had loved it. Not that the frozen snapper from the Staunton Valu-Mart would be as good as the fresh snapper she got at home in Baltimore, but she could still make it taste "like melted butter" as Thomas described it.

When the man approached her, she was taken by surprise and turned to see him standing next to her without hearing him come toward her.

"Can I help?" he asked.

"No, but thanks. I think I've got it now," she smiled and said just as she located her keys in her jeans pocket.

Suddenly she felt a pressure against her back and froze.

"Don't scream or I'll push this knife straight through your kidney." His voice was calm as if he were talking about the price of eggs.

Shawnette said nothing and looked forward and saw the green Buick parked there. Oh shit, she thought. Shit. Why didn't I see that?

"Walk forward to the passenger side of the Buick, open the door, put your bags in there and get in. I'll be behind you so if you try to run, you're dead. Now move."

She tried to think of running but he now had one hand firmly grasping her upper arm and she was afraid if she tried to take off he'd stab her before she could wrestle free.

"No. I'm going to scream. People will see you. You can hurt me. but you might not kill me. Too many people are around," she said, refusing to budge.

"Shawnette, do what I say or I will kill you and Thomas. I already have him in the trunk. Now stop thinking and move." He pushed her forward.

Thomas? How did he have Thomas in his trunk? How did he know their names? Who was this man? She became terribly afraid and just started moving without any thought except that he had said he had Thomas.

She did exactly as he instructed and slipped into the passenger seat, the knife still at her right side.

"Get those handcuffs out of the floor and put them on. And smile at me. Remember I have Thomas in the trunk. You don't want to do anything but what I say."

By the time she had locked the handcuffs on her wrists, she could hear him slamming the passenger door and coming round the front of the car. She was torn. She could really run right now and get away from him, but if he had Thomas in the trunk and he took off, Thomas could die.

In the few seconds that she took to think about what to do, he was already in the car.

"We're going to take a small trip. I want you to sit there and be quiet and smile. No talking. No screaming. Just sit and shut up."

They drove for longer than a "small trip." She felt as if an hour had passed and she wondered if Thomas could breathe in the trunk. Her imagination began to go a little off kilter and she wondered if he was hurt or bleeding. If he were bleeding, he could die if they didn't stop soon. She was so intent on thinking of Thomas in the trunk that the thought that neither one of them might not make it out of this did not occur to her.

It was fully dark by the time the car reached the dirt road off the Goshen exit and began to ascend the mountain. The headlights flashed against a no trespassing sign and Shawnette could see no other lights anywhere. The car came to a stop in front of an old single storey farmhouse.

"Get out and stand next to the car," he said. He came around behind her and knocked her forward. Just as she entered the dark front hall of the house, she felt something slam against the side of her head and she crumpled forward unconscious onto the floor.

---

Thomas was just climbing the steps of their apartment as Shawnette was falling to the floor. He was hungry and eager to see her. When he opened their door and saw the dark apartment, he wondered where she was. She had called on her cell and said she was going to the store and would meet him here in about an hour.

As he walked through the rooms turning on the lights and the TV, he began to wonder if she had

had car trouble. Sometimes her old Chevy wouldn't start and he had told her that he thought that they would need to replace the starter soon. She had said it would have to wait as long as they could until she could finish the semester and start her summer job at Penney's. He had reluctantly agreed, but only because they were trying to save money for a better place and the wedding she had always wanted.

He smiled as he thought of the ring box hidden behind the TV. He had picked it out three months ago and it had taken him that long to put the money together to buy it for her. He knew that practicality dictated that he put the money in the Chevy, but he wanted so much to see that brilliant smile of hers when he put the box in front of her. He was going to propose on Saturday night. He was taking her out to dinner as a surprise with the ring as the final surprise of the night.

As the ABC news went off and Jeopardy began, he was surprised to see that almost an hour had passed and she was not home yet. He took his cell out of his work shirt and pushed the button to call her. The phone instantly went to her voice mail, which told him that she was either out of range or that her phone was dead.

Two more hours of waiting and pacing went by before he decided to go look for her. The Valu-Mart was first on his list since she had called from there last. When he arrived there and saw her Chevy sitting in the lot with no cars around it, his throat tightened. He parked next to it and using his set of keys, opened it and tried to start it. It started without hesitation.

Where the hell was she?

---

She was waking up in the basement of the farm house just as Thomas was sitting in her car. She was sitting on the dirt in the dark and she could feel that she was completely naked with her hands trussed up above her. She tried to peer through the darkness and see if Thomas were there as well, but she could see nothing.

This was when she realized that she felt numb from the waist down as the other 10 women who had been brought here had felt except that she had no knowledge of them. She didn't realize that the foul odors in the basement were from twelve years of death and rot and dirt, but the smell made her gag slightly. The back of her head hurt, but not as much as her arms did where they burned from being held above her head for so long.

Upstairs, the man knew that Shawnette was probably awake now and he finished eating his meal of instant macaroni and cheese and fish sticks before heading downstairs with his tool kit. Over the years he had refined his techniques and now he had a kit with not only the necessary paralytic drugs, but also assorted knives, screwdrivers, needles and vises, not to mention his latest acquisition, a handheld rotary tool with all types of cutting wheels, tiny drills and grinding bits.

He had stalked Shawnette longer than he had watched any of the women he had brought here before and tonight he planned to make it a long night. He had planned all this so well and she was worth it all. She was a beauty and he planned to make her forget everything she had ever known except the pain he would bring her. The anticipation of all the things he could do with her made his penis ache.

In the past few years he had run extension cords into the basement that connected to shiny steel work lights that he had clamped on the beams above. The extra light made it so much better because he could see their expressions clearly as he worked.

He carried the kit with him and as he was walking along turning each light on and aiming it on her, she asked, "Where's Thomas? Is he ok?"

He stopped for a second and raised one eyebrow. Amazing, he thought. They always thought they were going to get away and this one, she was even more worried about her boyfriend than she was herself.

"I suppose he's home waiting for you. I have no idea."

She watched him undress and for the first time since she had seen his car, she took a full look at him. He was tanned and well built, slightly muscular arms but thin legs and a white boy's flat ass. Very dark hair that was lightly starting to grey at the temples. A handsome face. A face that she would have smiled at and would never have been afraid of. Until now, that was.

He opened his tool kit and when she saw his implements within it, she knew she was going to die. She began to quietly cry. Thomas wasn't coming. No one was coming. No last minute rescue like on TV. She was about to die and she knew it would be painful. She turned her head, closed her eyes and began to silently pray for her soul.

He jerked her head forward.

"Do not look away. If you turn your head, I will staple your hair to the pole. If you close your eyes, I'll remove your eyelids."

He squatted back on his haunches in front of her.

"It won't hurt for a while. For a while it will be fun. Lie back and enjoy it," he said and giggled like a girl.

He used the rotary tool to carve designs on her legs like a tattoo artist, drawing vines down and around her thighs, wiping the blood from the wounds with her shirt so he could admire his work.

After he completed his carving, he changed the tool bit to a flat cutting wheel and shoved it into her anus first. She could feel a slight pressure, but nothing more. He removed it and then pushed it into her vagina, whirling it around like a vibrator.

She looked down and could see blood pouring from her, but she still thanked God that she could not feel it. Nor did she feel it when he removed her clitoris with the cutting wheel, but when he took it and put it to the side; she began to gag, feeling the vomit rise in her throat.

He slapped her hard and said, "Do no throw up. I will remove your lips and tongue if you do."

She stared past him and focused on a bolt in the stairway so she would not see anymore of the obscenities he was performing on her body.

She could not stop the scream that emerged when began to use the grinding wheel on her breasts. And so he did as he had promised. He took a scalpel from the kit and removed her tongue and lips. Now all she could do was gurgle and groan as the blood formed a red brown bib on her breasts. By the time he had finished with her breasts, she was growing faint from the blood loss and he began slapping her to keep her awake.

As with the other women, she did not die until he had begun removing toes, fingers, then feet and wrists.

By the time she was dead, he completed his work by shoving his penis into her throat and jacking off.

"How about some Deep Throat, baby?" he asked the corpse of what had been Shawnette.

He felt great. It had been one hell of a night, he thought as the sun began to rise and he dressed to begin his clean-up routine.

This one had been the best. Ever.

# CHAPTER 21

*May 2010*

Trey was packing the Celica while Pea was standing off under the ancient maple tree across from the house. The sun filled the valley and the grass moved slightly in the wind as the shadows of the clouds sliding across the face of the sun scudded across the pasture.

"We're set now. Ready?"

She walked back to the car smiling.

"How can you leave here? It's so beautiful. I wouldn't want to ever leave," she said.

Those were words he wanted to hear from her, but he wasn't sure if she would be willing to leave her family farm to come here to live. Over the weekend he had begun to think of moving back into the house, bringing Pea with him to live there, and maybe, just maybe having a family.

He mentioned none of this to Pea. He was still too unsure of her fragile emotional state, especially concerning the ghosts that held her to the Greenbrier Valley. He had watched her sleeping last night and felt in her a peace and quiet that he had not seen since he had met her.

Secrets, she had asked. Yes, he had secrets. Didn't everyone, he thought? But nothing they couldn't face together. With her he felt as if he could face his own ghosts that he had been running from for over a decade.

They had almost reached Lexington when she mentioned again that she needed to go home to check on the farm. He nodded that he understood. She had things to think about.

He believed that although she had told him she loved him that she might not be able to make a commitment to him and there was also the fact that he had not asked her to do so. After almost three months together, he knew he loved her, but he was not sure that that had been enough time for her. There was so much that she seemed to be holding back. She might need longer and he was willing to wait if necessary.

"Ree's graduation is next week. I'd like you to meet her before then, both she and Joseph," she said. "I know I've put it off, but for the life of me I couldn't tell you why."

He looked over at her as the cars passed them on the interstate.

"It's not you. It was never you. You believe me, don't you?"

He nodded yes, that he believed her. He hadn't been happy about it, but he knew it was one more thing she had to work out. It just frustrated him endlessly that she wouldn't allow him to help her through any of it.

"I'll be back late Tuesday night. Ree has finals all week so maybe on Friday we can get together with them?"

He thought about the meal for a moment.

"I can cook if you'd like. It'd be a lot more informal than a restaurant and we could all take more time, relax, get to know one another," he offered.

What he didn't say, but thought, was that Pea would be more relaxed. Either way, it seemed the easiest way to him.

"Yes, of course. That would be great. A restaurant would be a bit stiff and Ree and Joseph's apartment is way too small for even the four of us. Tiny kitchen and no dining room, though Ree is a great cook."

He laughed. "Yes, I know. She got the cooking gene."

"I can't be perfect in everything," she said laughing with him.

"Oh, I can think of a few things you're damned near perfect at," he said and reached over to squeeze her hand.

"I know," she said and laughed again.

As they exited I-81, she saw the Horse Center and her mood fell immediately and for the first time she realized the staff there would be preparing for the opening show of the season. When she drove from Greenbrier County, the exit was away from the Center and she never saw it, but coming from Staunton, it loomed large as they exited the interstate. She could feel her breathing beginning to increase and her heart race. It was suddenly very warm in the car and she felt herself growing dizzy.

Trey had heard her breaths increase and he glanced over at her. He then saw the Horse Center right in front of them and for the first time in years, he ran a red light trying to get her away from there so he could find a place to pull the Celica over. About a half mile from the Center, he pulled into an empty bank parking lot, looked back and saw that the Center was now obscured by trees.

"Pea, lean forward and close your eyes. Try to concentrate on my voice and not think of anything else but the sound of my voice."

She leaned forward as he spoke and focused on his voice. She wasn't sure what he was saying, but she could feel his hand stroking her back. When she had seen the Horse Center, she had been thinking of how happy she had been for the past few months and then seeing it was as if someone had slapped her in the face, saying "How dare you be happy when you killed your child?"

The panic attack was not passing quickly enough and all she could think of was getting to her sister's. She was beginning to struggle for each breath and no amount of comfort from Trey seemed to help.

Somehow, she managed to get out her sister's name. "Ree's," she gasped.

He pulled back onto the street and headed into town towards the university. By the time he had reached Mary's apartment, the panic attack had overwhelmed her.

# CHAPTER 22

The pounding on the door took Joseph by surprise and he hesitated before opening the door. He did not recognize the man standing there, a man who appeared to quite frantic.

"Is Ree here?" the man asked.

Joseph paused in confusion and then realized he meant Mary.

"Uh, yes, just a minute," and he turned towards the bedroom calling Mary's name.

She entered the room and the man at the door said, "Pea. She's in trouble. She's in the car. I can't seem to help."

Before he could even finish his sentence, Mary had pushed past him and was heading downstairs. By the time the two men had descended the steps, they saw that Mary had the passenger door open and was holding Pea, whispering softly to her. She finally soothed Pea enough to lead her from the car to the apartment as both men watched helplessly.

Mary led Pea up the stairs and took her into the bedroom and closed the door between the men and the sisters.

Trey sat down on the chair next to the door and hung his head in exhaustion.

"I didn't know what else to do. She just said "Ree's" and this was all I could think to do."

Joseph told him to come with him and silently made a pot of fresh coffee, pouring three cups and offering one to Trey.

"What happened?" Joseph asked quietly.

Trey looked up and ran his hand through his hair. He actually wasn't quite sure. He told Joseph that they had spent the weekend at his family place north of Staunton and that things had been great until they took the Lexington exit when she started to have a panic attack.

"I think it was the Horse Center. She did say Alicia's name. That and "Ree's" was the most I could get out of her."

He sat up straight for a minute and looked toward the closed bedroom door. "God, is she going to be ok? She's still so fragile."

Joseph took a deep drink of his coffee. He wasn't sure what had happened and he frowned.

He knew that Pea was much stronger than she appeared, but then he also knew that he could not allow either Mary or Trey to know that he knew this.

They sat with their unspoken thoughts for almost 10 minutes before Mary came through the bedroom door, closing it softly as she did. She walked straight to Joseph and took the coffee cup he offered up to her. She stared at Trey for a moment trying to decide if she approved of him and Trey could feel that in her stare.

"Sit down, Mary. Tell us what's wrong," Joseph said placing his hand on her back,

"Trey?" she asked. He said yes.

"I'm Mary, or Ree as Pea calls me. This is Joseph."

She paused and then continued.

"I had hoped to meet you before today, but not because of what happened. In fact, I'm ashamed to admit that I had forgotten the date. If I had remembered . . . I've been studying and it slipped my mind."

"How could I be so stupid?" She slumped on the couch against Joseph.

"What are you talking about?" Trey asked.

Mary sat forward again and took a deep breath. "Today is the third anniversary of Alicia's death. I think the sight of the Horse Center set the panic attack off. I think even she may have forgotten the date and when she remembered, the guilt overcame her."

She faced Trey and said, "I was there when Alicia died. I was there for her the past three years, including the last year of her marriage to that son of a bitch."

Trey hung his head again and once more was pushing his hand through his hair.

Joseph, on the other hand, felt as if he were watching a play from the audience. He knew Pea was stronger than this, but it was also something he couldn't reveal to Mary or Trey. Now he understood what had happened. Alicia was the chink in the armor Pea had been building the past three years. It made sense.

"Shit," Trey cursed under his breath. "I didn't know. She never told me the date or I might, I might have . . ." his voice trailed off.

"Trey, she did not cause Alicia's death. A fool with a firecracker behind the stands spooked Blondie and the horse reared. Alicia lost her grip and felt off, breaking her neck. That bastard Manley told her it was her fault because she hadn't tightened all the straps, but she had. He might as well have beaten her with the guilt he threw at her every day for a year while he was out sleeping with anything that moved. The fucking bastard. But she did not kill her daughter."

Joseph began to rub Mary's neck, trying to calm her now.

"But Pea told me it was because she hadn't tightened the straps correctly," Trey said.

"No, that's what Manley told her. I was there. I saw her check the straps three times. If you know Pea at all, you know she checks things over and over again," Mary said.

Trey didn't know what to say or do. He looked at Joseph rubbing Mary's neck.

"Did I cause this?" he finally asked.

Mary shook her head. "Absolutely not. Taking her out of town was probably the best thing you could have done." She paused again and took another sip of her coffee. Joseph rose and brought the coffee pot into the living room and refilled their cups.

"If she could just understand that she has nothing to feel guilty about. I've been trying for three years to get her to stop. She just locked herself on that farm. Nothing has worked."

Then she looked up at Trey and said, "At least until she met you. She's seemed better the past three months."

She looked at Joseph who had sat back down on the sofa next to her. He knew where she was going and he closed his eyes. He wanted her to stop, but he knew that trying to stop her would be futile.

"Are you serious about her? If you're not, you need to let her go now. She can't take losing someone again," Mary said firmly.

Trey was surprised by her frankness and about to reply when Joseph said, "Stop it, Mary. Stop now."

"Let the man breathe for a moment. Just stop." He took her hand and held it tightly.

Trey sat back for a moment and stared back at Mary just as defiantly as she stared at him.

"I love her. Now, if you don't mind, I'm going in there and check on her." He stood, but stopped halfway across the room. "She's not alone anymore. I'm not going anywhere. But don't come at me like that again. I came here for help for her, not to dump her in your bedroom. That should tell you something."

He went into the bedroom and Mary leaned against Joseph.

"Why can't I keep my mouth shut?" she asked.

"Because you love her. And, because you have no censor on that beautiful mouth of yours. But it's also why I love you so much," he replied as she snuggled against him and began to cry.

## CHAPTER 23

Pea was no longer weeping. She was lying on her side on the bed staring at the tiny violets on the wall paper. When Trey came in and sat down on the bed next to her, she continued to stare forward.

"Ree and your mother have the same wallpaper."

Trey looked around the room and recognized the pattern as the same one at his parents' home.

"Yes, it seems they do." He gently put his hand on her hip.

"I'm sorry about this evening. Ree says I apologize too much, but I think I truly owe you an apology for this," she said.

"Can you scoot over?" he asked.

She moved to the middle of the bed as he stretched out next to her, his face close to hers.

"You owe no one anything. You had a bad time and I didn't know about the date. I brought you here because I thought Mary could help you because I didn't understand."

She stroked his cheek and wanted to kiss him for such kindness.

"Why are you still here?" she asked. "Most men would have been running in the opposite direction by now. I'm a mess. A useless mess."

"I'm here because I love you. I thought that you saw that this weekend, but maybe not. It doesn't matter anyway. I still love you and I'll keep saying it and maybe you'll believe me one day."

She sighed and curled her body against his.

"Can you take me home?"

"To your farm?"

"No, to your house. I want to go home with you, that is if you still want me."

"I still want you. Get up and we'll go."

She rose from the bed and went toward the bathroom to splash water on her face and try to compose herself.

"I love you, Pea," he said, but he wasn't sure if she could hear him.

When they opened the bedroom door, Joseph was holding Mary against his chest. She immediately stood and went to Pea. She knew that

Pea was going home with Trey. They both looked better now, though the worry still creased his brow.

"Are you going to be ok tonight?"

Pea hugged her sister and said yes. She looked over to Joseph and apologized to him. Joseph came over to where the three of them stood.

"Mary is right about one very important thing," he said. "You have to stop saying you're sorry so much. You asked me once if I could live through what you have and I never answered you. But the truth is, I don't know. You've been through more in two or three years than anyone should have to go through. But, as Mary and Trey keep telling you, none of it is your fault." He hugged her and then held her at arm's length.

"You're much stronger than you know."

Trey led Pea out the door to his Celica and Mary watched them leave from the front window. It would be a few days before she realized what Joseph had said and that she had no idea of what he meant or why he said it. But by then, their time together would be growing shorter than she could possibly know.

# CHAPTER 24

Instead of going back to the Greenbrier Valley, Pea called Mr. Dickson to check on the animals and asked him to make sure everything was ok with the house. She told him she wasn't sure when she would be back because of Mary's upcoming graduation.

A pang hit her thinking of her dogs waiting for her patiently. She missed them more than she missed the farm and that surprised her as the farm had been the center of her existence for the past decade.

She had told Trey that she was driving home and he had insisted that he go with her, but she demurred, saying that she needed the time alone. She was still very embarrassed by her panic attack on the anniversary of Alicia's death. It was the first time she had not gone to Alicia's grave to place fresh daisies there for her. She felt guilty for that and she felt guilty for leaving Trey and lying to him about where she was going, but she knew the only way for her to pass through this time was to place her thoughts as far away from the past as possible.

So, instead of going home, she drove to Staunton again to meet Thomas Washington and Joseph. The three of them were going to try to retrace Shawnette's last few weeks by the places she had mentioned in her journal. Maybe they could find the green Buick somewhere along the routes Shawnette and the other women had taken. They only had the one day and they needed every second of it to cover the area.

She met them both outside of Thomas's apartment and they took Joseph's Taurus instead of Thomas's truck or her small Audi. The Taurus was much less inconspicuous and held the three of them comfortably. Pea sat quietly in the back, talking little and trying to concentrate on the cars and parking lots they passed. Actually, not any of them said much for the entirety of the morning. Their minds were all elsewhere even if they had set this task for themselves today.

Joseph kept thinking of Mary taking her exams today, worrying himself with the same nagging thoughts of their impending separation. He felt that his lies about what he was doing did little to help his situation.

Thomas could think of nothing but the police pictures of Shawnette's body. Joseph had tried to hide the photographs from him, but he had found them over the weekend when neither Pea nor Joseph was at the office. The pictures had broken him. Unknown to Pea and Joseph, he had lost his will and strength. He slumped against the window, chewing on a toothpick and trying to decide whether he even wanted to continue living anymore. He was on the brink of suicide and only the thought of possibly finding the man who had mutilated his beautiful Shawnette's body kept him breathing.

Pea's silence was linked closely to Joseph's. The lying to Trey and Mary was making her feel as if she were about to lose everything again and that she would find herself back at the farm, alone and old and unloved by anyone. As for Alicia's death and Pea's breakdown on Sunday, she tried to black it out of her mind entirely.

And it was because these preoccupations were so strongly overpowering them that they failed to see the green Buick parked on a side street near the Episcopal Church cemetery in the center of Staunton. But the man in the Buick saw them and he recognized two of them and he was suddenly filled with fear for the first time in 12 years.

What the fuck were they doing together? A voice inside his head was screaming. How did they even know each other and what the fuck was she doing away from her farm? He did not like this and he backed the car down the alley and headed out toward Rt. 11 to avoid their seeing him.

They were also seen by a second driver who watched them drive by the old Staunton Train Station. The driver was so stunned to see them that he at first thought he was seeing someone else and not Pea. But instead of fleeing, he followed them until he saw them pull up to a dry cleaner's and park. He watched as the three of them exited the car and headed into the building.

And he, too, wondered what the hell was going on? Why was she with them? What were they doing? None of it made sense to him.

He sat outside the building for almost 30 minutes before he decided to leave. He was angry, but not nearly as angry as the other driver. He, too, headed for Rt. 11 and swallowed the urge to go back and confront them.

Meanwhile, the three of them were discussing their very fruitless search. Joseph pointed out that the whole thing seemed very well unlikely for them to solve. He, and they, had found no connections and he felt they should end their search.

Pea angrily fought him at every turn. She was not giving up. They had come too far. The answer had to be there. There had to be a connection between the 12 women that they had missed.

Thomas just sat slumped on his couch, staring out the window, silent.

"Thomas, don't you think we should do this one last thing? Thomas?"

He turned to look at Pea and Joseph and covered his eyes with his hand. He needed this to stop so much. He truthfully didn't know how much more he could take.

"Look, this is just a hunt for you two," he said. "But I've lost everything. Do you understand that? Everything."

He took a deep breath and exhaled slowly.

"I'll go back to Lexington with you one more time and look at everything again, but I'm done. I can't stop thinking about Shawnette's legs and her . . ." His voice broke at that point and he bowed his head, holding his hands to his face.

Pea moved over to him and knelt before him.

Joseph said, "You found the photographs."

"Yes, I found the fucking photographs. I saw what the monster did to her," and he began to weep.

Pea took her hands and placed them on his, pulling his head against her shoulder and let him weep. She had never seen a man cry before, not even Manley when Alicia had died. But she knew the pain of losing the most important thing in your life and she didn't think that kind of pain did not transcend sexes.

Joseph now turned away and looked out the window at the late afternoon. He could not know what either of them felt at that moment. The horror of both their lives was both familiar and alien to him. He had spent years of his life with grieving families, but he had only compassion and empathy to offer them. He could never understand the depth of the pain they felt.

After a while, Thomas lifted his head from Pea's shoulder and looked into her blue eyes. He saw his own pain reflected there and for the first time in a year felt that someone might understand his despair. Somewhere deep inside of him he had stupidly thought that maybe the body they had found wasn't really Shawnette and that she would walk through the door one night. He had thought that until last weekend when he found the photographs and then he knew that she was gone.

"You know I've never been to Shawnette's grave. I should have. I should have. I just never wanted to believe that she was really gone."

Pea moved from the floor and sat next to him on the sofa. She looked toward Joseph who was still gazing out the window.

"I've done nothing but spend the last few years going to my daughter's grave. Going there every day has nearly destroyed me," she said.

She smoothed her skirt against her legs and spoke to both of them. Joseph watched her carefully, trying to decipher the emotions on her face.

"I should have thought about all of this before pushing it all into each of your lives. It was my selfish attempt to get past my pain without thinking of what it would do to you two. I was wrong. I was so wrong.

Before Joseph could speak, Thomas did.

"No. No, you were, are right. I was sitting here waiting for Shawnette to come home. I wouldn't even allow myself to grieve and Shawnette deserved so much more than what I've done."

Joseph sat forward in the chair.

"I think we should go back to the office and look at everything again. Go and see what we might have missed. Do you still want to pursue this? If either of you want out now, we need to do it now."

"And Pea, we have to tell Mary and Trey. I can't hide this from her anymore. I know she's going to leave soon anyway and I would like to spend what little time we have left together with no secrets."

She reached over and took Joseph's hand.

"Mary's not leaving you, Joseph. She's not. I know."

He gave her a small sad smile and said, "Well, we'll see."

"We should get on the road," and he stood and began to pull on his blazer as Pea and Thomas rose to leave as well.

Outside the apartment in the tiny space he had used to watch Shawnette, the man waited for them to exit. He had some idea of where they were going, but he was going to go there first.

# CHAPTER 25

While the three of them had arrived back in Lexington and went to the spare office, Mary was walking across campus when she saw a green Buick parked outside her apartment. The driver was watching the building and he did not see her approach the car. When she saw his face, she filled with anger.

"What the hell are you doing here?" She jerked the door of the Buick open and the driver was stunned to find he had been discovered.

"Why are you here?" Mary demanded.

He looked around and began to be afraid of others hearing her raised voice and seeing him. Without thinking he punched her in the face and knocked her to the ground, her books falling to the ground beside her as blood began to flow from her broken nose and busted lip.

Before she could react, he grabbed her and shoved her into the car, punching her in the head this time and driving her into unconsciousness.

Oh, this was fucked up, he thought, but he knew where and what he needed to do and the first thing was to escape from here.

---

Pea, Thomas and Joseph were going through each of the files again and Pea moved from the table to the wall. She began to see a pattern she had missed. There. And there. How had they missed those? How had she missed those?

"I think I have something." The two men looked up from their files and to the wall.

"Pearl Montgomery, the victim with my name, disappeared on my birthday."

"The next victim was Mattie. She disappeared a year later, about a week before my wedding."

"Each of the victims all disappeared around events in my life. And here, look, one of them was even name Alice Marie. She died a few weeks after my daughter died."

"We've been looking for a common denominator in the wrong places. The common denominator was so simple that we didn't think of it because you two didn't realize the importance of the dates. Mary would have seen it and God knows I should have. God, I should have."

"Now look at the dates - they're all clustered between the end of May and the first weeks of June. And," she said as she moved to the map, "The first women were never found. It's as if as he got more adept at killing that he wanted people to see his work. Shawnette, the 11th woman, was very openly left to be found. It was his way of saying "See me. I'm here." Don't serial killers do that, Joseph? Get bolder and want more recognition?"

Both men were staring at the wall as if everything began to fall into focus.

"Don't you see?" she said. "I'm the common denominator."

# CHAPTER 26

Joseph sat in stunned silence, trying to assimilate everything she had just said.

She was right. All the deaths had focused around her and events in her life. She had done it again. She had seen the pattern where no one else had.

Thomas spoke up. He was beginning to see something about what Pea was saying, but he had not made the central connection as she and Joseph had.

"But why Shawnette or any of these women? Even if the events point toward events in your life, what do these women have to do with it?"

Joseph froze with fear as a thought entered his mind. The person they were looking for was someone Pea already knew, someone Mary knew.

And it was an anniversary week which meant that he was going to kill again.

"Oh, God, Pea, Mary. We've got to get to the apartment. I have to make sure she's ok."

Pea was stricken by what he was saying. They both knew who the killer was. They ran to the door and Thomas followed, still not sure what was happening.

By the time Joseph had reached the apartment building ahead of them, he saw the books on the sidewalk and almost fell on them. He grabbed one and saw Mary's name written inside the flyleaf. He sat on the sidewalk and could not catch his breath. It was when he saw the blood on the sidewalk that the pains in his chest and arm began.

"Mary, Pea, he's got her." Joseph could barely breathe. He felt like an anvil had been pushed onto his chest and he couldn't speak. The color began to drain from his face and he fell back onto the sidewalk.

Pea grabbed her cell and hit 911.

"Hold on Joseph. Hold on. Help is coming." She lifted his head onto her lap and took his hand. "We'll find her. We'll find her. She's going to be ok. Just hold on."

She looked up at Thomas. "My sister. He's taken my sister. I need your help. I need you to get someone and bring them to the hospital. Please. I need them."

Pea gave him the information he needed and he started to run down the hill toward town just as the ambulance pulled up to the curb.

Pea clasped Joseph tighter. "Stay with me Joseph. Mary won't forgive me if I let something happen to you."

Joseph opened his eyes for a moment and tried to smile before passing out from the pain.

# CHAPTER 27

Trey was almost as surprised to see the tall black man standing at his door as he had been to see Pea with the man and Joseph in Staunton.

He was still very, very angry and almost closed the door in the man's face, but the man pushed against the door and stopped him.

Thomas was out of breath. He had just run almost a mile to Trey's house and he didn't have time for this asshole.

"Trey Thornton. Is he here? I need to speak with him. It's an emergency."

Trey stepped out onto the stoop.

"I'm Trey. Who are you?"

Thomas bent over, putting his hands on his knees, trying to get his breath.

"Pea sent me. We think . . . Joseph is having a heart attack. She's gone with him to the hospital." Thomas managed to get the words out between gasps.

Trey grabbed his coat and keys from inside the door.

"My car is over here. Were they taking him to Lexington Memorial?"

Thomas nodded as he got into the Celica. He was concerned that they could be losing precious time in figuring out where Mary was.

"Did Pea call Mary?" Trey asked.

Thomas realized that he had not told Trey everything. "Mary's been taken. We found her books on the sidewalk outside her building. Joseph and Pea seem to know who has taken her, but they didn't have a chance to tell me before he started having the heart attack."

Trey stared at Thomas in shock.

"What do you mean Mary's been taken? By whom? Has she been kidnapped?"

Thomas shook his head. "Not kidnapped." He was finally starting to catch his breath. "Taken. By a serial killer. I don't know who, but they seemed to have figured it out and they took off running for Pea's sister's place. That's when we found the books and Pea sent me for you."

"I can't believe this. I don't even know what you're talking about. A serial killer? In Lexington?"

Thomas told him that Pea would be better able to explain it than he could. He said he wasn't sure of what she and Joseph had figured out.

But, if it meant they knew who had killed Shawnette, there was no force on earth that would stop him from finding the sick fuck, he thought.

Trey found Pea standing outside of a door looking into a room of the Lexington Memorial ER. She was watching whatever was happening in the room, her arms crossed against her chest, her face pale.

"Pea, are you alright? Is Joseph? What's going on?"

The woman who turned to face him was a woman he had never really seen before. Her face was hard and angry. Worried, yes, but not the fragile, sometimes happy and sometimes broken woman he had known for the past three months. But she reached out to him and hugged him hard, grasping him like she was about to sink.

"Trey, I've done something so stupid. I have to fix this and I need you right now. If you want out afterwards, I'll understand. I should have told you months ago."

He led Pea over to chairs outside the door and sat down next to her as Thomas moved to the window and watched as the ER team worked on Joseph. Thomas thought Joseph looked worse and wondered if he would survive this. This was bad and something bad was what he had felt this whole search had been leading to.

Behind him, he could hear Pea describing the events of the past few months, the search, the meetings, Joseph's profiling and even Thomas's role in the whole mess. He glanced at them and saw that Trey was not dealing with this very well. He could understand that. He had told both Pea and Joseph from the start that they should not keep this from Mary or Trey, but they didn't listen.

He knew from Shawnette's experience, from her failure to tell him about her fears, the stalking, all of it had led to her death. His head told him that he might not have been able to have stopped the killer, but his heart told him he should have. And he knew that when it came to someone you loved, the heart always had the first and last say.

Thomas turned to them and saw that Pea was looking at the doors and Trey would not look at her. He could see a flood of emotions cross Trey's face and he felt sorry for this man. The woman he thought he knew was someone else. Never something that was easily accepted.

Finally Trey turned to Pea. "You should have told me."

"You would have tried to stop me, just as Mary did." She took a deep breath. "Oh, god, Mary, we've got to go get her. We've got to get there before . . . "

Thomas had been about to ask where as the doors behind him opened and a doctor emerged to speak with them.

"Mr. Hallett has suffered a minor heart attack, but we haven't found any significant damage to his heart. He had a small blockage and we're preparing him to go straight to the heart cath lab. After that, he's going to have to stay here for at least three to five days for observation and as much rest as possible. Under no circumstances is he to be overexcited or overexert himself."

"Can we talk to him?" Pea stood and asked.

"Only one at a time right now. We'll be moving him upstairs in the next few hours."

As the doctor walked away from them, Pea did not hesitate in opening the door and heading to Joseph.

Trey and Thomas watched her as she took Joseph's hand and spoke to him. They could see him nodding and then shaking his head. He dropped her hand, said something, and then pointed at Trey. Pea nodded and walked to the door.

"He wants to talk to you, Trey," she said as she went back to the chair.

While Trey went in to talk to Joseph, Thomas sat down next to Pea.

"So, where are we going? I know you have an idea of where he is."

She nodded. He watched her face and saw that her eyes were dry, her face calm and set.

"You know I'm going to stop him for good," Thomas said staring at Pea.

She nodded again and looked down at her hands, turning them over as if searching for something she had lost.

"Joseph doesn't want me to go. He's in there telling Trey to call the FBI and the police. He's telling Trey to get me out of it," she said.

"I can't do that, Thomas. Mary is gone because of my blindness. And I may be the only one he might trade for Mary. I can't let her die for me. I can't and I won't." She stood and gazed into the window again. Trey nodded his head and began to walk to the doors. Pea stepped back and waited.

"Where is she?" Trey asked.

"Pea, tell me. We can't do this. You can't."

She lifted her chin defiantly, another expression he had never really noticed before, but one that Thomas had seen often.

"She's not going to just let you call the FBI," Thomas said.

Trey turned angrily to Thomas and said, "Well, then what the hell do we do? Just let the bastard torture and kill Mary? Or get Pea killed as well? Is that what you're saying?"

He pushed a finger at Thomas's chest and Thomas grew angry as well and started to put his hand on Trey's shoulder, but before he could, Pea slipped between them.

"Stop it. Both of you." She looked to Trey. "I'm going to get my sister. Come with me or not, but I'm going."

She paused and for a brief second her face softened.

"I love you, Trey Thornton, but I cannot let my sister die for me. Please forgive my lapses, my not telling you, but I've got to go now. I'm sorry," she said and walked away from him toward the exit.

Thomas pushed past Trey and followed Pea down the hall.

"Oh, shit." Trey said quietly and then ran after the two of them, reaching them just as they exited the ER, the sliding doors whooshing closed behind him.

"Since I'm the only one here with a car, someone needs to tell me where I'm driving," he said and headed towards his car.

# CHAPTER 28

"Goshen," Pea said as they pulled out of the hospital parking lot.

"Once you take the exit, turn north and there's a dirt road with a cattle gate about three miles from the exit. That's the road we need."

Thomas sat in the back seat of the Celica and watched them both, unyielding and yet unstoppable. She would not give up and Trey would not let her go alone. And both of them were furious. So furious that they wouldn't even look at one another.

And for some unfathomable reason, he started to laugh, a laugh that he had not heard in over a year and a laugh that was so hard that it made his sides hurt.

Trey looked at him in the rear view mirror as if he had lost his mind and Pea turned around in the seat and reached her hand out to him.

"Thomas."

"Thomas, are you ok?"

Tears streaked his dark skin and he still could not stop laughing. Oh, Shawnette, honey. I'm too late, but I'll try to fix this, he thought.

"Yes," he said wiping his face against his sleeve. "Ok."

"Ok."

"You two. You . . ." his voice trailed off. They wouldn't understand even if he tried to explain it to them.

Pea was puzzled, but turned back to face forward in the passenger seat. This time she looked over at Trey and he returned her gaze, a small acknowledgement that at least comforted Pea somewhat.

They reached the dirt road almost an hour after they had left the house. Thomas reckoned that at least four to five hours had passed since Mary had been taken. They might still have a chance. He might not have started to torture her yet. Thomas closed his eyes and prayed to God that he had not started yet. Be with her Shawnette, Thomas thought. Help her through it if he has and I'll help you find peace, he promised.

Trey drove down the road about a mile before the road began to steepen and he stopped the Celica there.

"There used to be a one-storey farm house at the top of this rise, about half a mile from here," Pea said.

Trey peered into the darkness. There was only starlight above them and the terrain looked rough.

"I don't think we should drive up to the house. He might hear the car and we don't know what we're going into. And the hillside's no good. He might have traps set up," he said.

Thomas didn't wait to discuss it any further. He got out of the car and started to walk slowly up the hill. Trey and Mary scrambled out of the car behind him, following him up the hill.

"Wait," Trey hissed. "Wait!"

Thomas turned to them.

"I've waited a over a year," he whispered. "I'm done waiting."

Pea grabbed his arm and said, "Listen, he's going to expect at least two of us, but he won't expect Trey. He's probably waiting for you and me, Thomas. Maybe even outside. So we have to decide how to do this and not get ourselves or Mary killed."

Thomas agreed and pushed his anger back a bit.

"I'm going first. I'm lighter and I'll be quieter. I know my way around the property. I can head back up the hillside instead of the road and circle the house to the back door."

"Absolutely not," Trey said just as Thomas said "No" as well.

"Listen," she said. "If Thomas goes down the road first and he's focused on the road, he won't see me. I can get Mary out and meet you halfway down the hill. Just divert his attention."

"And what if that doesn't work? What if he's armed? What if he expects a trick?" Trey said.

Pea shook her head.

"He won't. He'll see two people which is what he would expect if he thinks Thomas and I have figured out he's here. Stay in the shadows and he won't be able to tell who the people are and he'll keep watching you. He won't hear or see me."

"No," both men said again, but Pea ran across the field and up the hill before either of them could say another word.

Trey didn't know whether to chase her or do as she said. It made sense, but he couldn't let her go off alone. It was against everything his heart was telling him.

Thomas touched his arm and whispered, "Let's go."

As they walked up the road, Thomas kicked at a rock here and there and hit overhanging branches with his hand. He figured that making noise on the road might mask any sound Pea might make clambering up the hillside.

Within one hundred yards of the house, they could see lights on inside and the green Buick parked outside. They both stopped. They stood in the shadows, waiting. Trey was praying that Pea had made it safely up the hillside to the back door. He couldn't stand here waiting. This was stupid, he thought, and he moved from the shadows into the light cast from the house.

Thomas moved next to him and whispered, "Are you crazy? Get out of this light."

Before he finished saying the word "light", they both heard the report of a rifle. Thomas looked at his shoulder and then at Trey as a second shot echoed through the hollow. Trey grabbed Thomas by the arm and pulled him back into the shadows.

"Are you shot?" he asked Thomas.

Thomas nodded. "He got my shoulder and knee."

Trey took off his shirt and using a pocket knife, ripped the side seam to pull a strip of cloth from it to tie around Thomas's leg. He tore more strips and used them on both Thomas's knee and shoulder.

Thomas groaned a bit and then stopped Trey.

"You've got to go find her. Find them. He won't expect you. She was right."

"This is right?" Trey asked

Thomas smiled and then grimaced. "Partially right, at least. Now go. Go."

Pea was at the back door of the house when she heard the gunshots. She slipped in the back door and almost tripped over Mary's unconscious body tied to the kitchen radiator pipe. She desperately looked around for a something to cut Mary's ropes with when she spied the kit on the table, open with a buck knife lying on top of the contents. She crawled over to the table, reached up, grabbed the knife and scuttled back to where Mary lay. Just as she cut the ropes, Mary began to stir.

"Shhh. Mary. Come on. We've got to get out of here. Be very quiet. He has a gun."

Mary rubbed the back of her head and started to say something, but Pea put her hand over Mary's mouth. "Shhh. He'll hear us," she said as she helped Mary to her feet.

"Yes, I will hear you."

Pea looked up and her eyes burned with hatred. "Hello, Manley."

## CHAPTER 29

"You know, I would never have thought you would have been smart enough to find me here." He had the gun loosely aimed at them and was relaxed as he spoke.

"You were always such a stupid cunt. I could see Mary possibly putting it together. Is that what happened? Did Mary figure it out?"

Mary was still leaning against Pea and Pea carefully slipped the buck knife into the loose pocket of her skirt. Mary rubbed her head again and shook it.

"Fuck you, Manley. Did you not think that I hadn't found your hidden land and house that you bought with my money? I followed you here before the divorce," she said.

He laughed at her response and looked at Pea. He saw a different woman there in her eyes.

"So how did you get it, little Pearl? And just what do you know?"

"I know all of it," she hissed. "I know about all 12 of the women, that you're a sick . . . sick motherfucker, that you tortured those women before you murdered them. I should have realized how sick you were 12 years ago, you and your sick relationship with your mother."

His face darkened and he raised the gun.

"Leave my mother out of it, cunt."

"Oh, please, Manley, shoot me. You may think you ruined my life, but you failed. You failed," she said as she pushed Mary behind her and closer to the back door.

He lowered the gun slightly and watched them, trying to anticipate how to get them into the basement. He had figured that Mary would be the difficult one, but he was finding Pea more aggressive than he expected.

"No, that wouldn't be very much fun. I think instead that we're going to move this downstairs."

"And don't expect any help. Whoever else was out there is dead. Two shots. Two down. Two to go," he added laughing.

Pea had moved forward as she had pushed Mary toward the back door, still making sure that her body blocked his shot at Mary.

She had to get Mary out of there.

"No. Shoot me. I'm not afraid of you. You will get no more satisfaction from hurting me. Not emotionally. Not physically, you bastard."

"Oh, Pea, you are so funny. Did you think that I ever cared about you or your brat? Watching you watch her die after I undid the saddle strap was the best revenge I had for putting up with you and that fucking farm."

Pea suddenly felt as if she had been hit hard in the gut.

"You killed Alicia? Our daughter? How could you?"

"The brat stood between me and your money. If she had been born a male, she might have been spared. But probably not. You really are such a stupid cunt. I never wanted any part of you but the money," he said.

Mary was completely conscious by this time and was aware of what Pea had been trying to do, but she knew she couldn't allow Pea to die for her. She rushed past Pea toward Manley, but he punched her in the stomach hard with the rifle, knocking her to the floor.

Outside the open front door, Trey had heard everything and was trying think of some way to stop this horrible nightmare from playing out. But, before he had the chance to act, Pea did something unthinkable.

She walked up to the barrel of the gun and began to cry.

"Manley, I loved you. Can't you at least think of what we had once? Please. I'll go with you back to the farm. You can do what you want to me there. Just leave Mary here to walk back to the highway. We'll be long gone by then. Please?"

She was holding the barrel of the rifle with both hands now.

Trey was afraid to breathe or make a sound. The rifle was so close to her. He feared that Manley would shoot her if he heard anything.

Manley hesitated for a second and in that second Pea moved to the side and tried to grab the gun from him, but she was not quite quick enough. He swung the barrel at her head, but she was fast enough to duck.

Just as she was bringing the buck knife from her skirt pocket and aiming it Manley's chest, Trey burst through the open doorway from his hiding place and grabbed Manley's arms. As Manley turned toward Trey, Pea plunged the knife up into Manley's chest. As he fell to the ground, she continued stabbing him until Trey pulled her away as he grabbed the gun off the floor.

"The bastard. The bastard killed my child. The bastard."

"Pea, stop. Stop, Pea! He's dead. He's gone."

She stopped and looked at Manley's bloody body and then at Trey. She pulled away from Trey and turned to help Mary from the floor, heading for the front door.

"Is Thomas alive?" She stopped without turning to face Trey.

"Yes, but he needs to get to a hospital soon.

She threw her cell phone to him and said, "Call the police and an ambulance. I'm taking Mary out of here."

Pea half carried Mary out of the house and walked down the front steps to where Thomas lay. She stopped there and they sat on the dirt road in the cool spring air. She looked up and saw the Milky Way spreading across the sky. She was still watching the starlit sky when Trey came outside to sit next to her.

# CHAPTER 30

It was almost dawn by the time that the police and ambulances had arrived. The ambulances would take Thomas and Mary to Lexington. Pea climbed in the back of the ambulance with Mary and refused to budge. As the ambulance pulled away from the house and headed down the dirt road, she saw Trey standing with the police, watching as she left with her sister.

Later, it would take Joseph and the four of them to explain everything that had happened to them that night as well as the deaths of the 12 women.

Mary was diagnosed with a mild concussion and given orders to spend the night in a hospital room, but she refused. Pea had informed her of Joseph's heart attack and she left the emergency room to search for him. She found him in the Cardiac Care Unit and would not leave his bedside.

When he opened his eyes that morning to find Mary sitting next to him, holding his hand with bruises covering her beautiful face, he was worried but still relieved that she had survived.

She related the events of the past day to him, including Pea's courage in facing Manley as well as Manley's admission to the murders of the women. She also began to discuss his recuperation at her family farm and said that whatever plans they would make could be made then.

For the first time, Joseph saw that his worries about losing Mary were unfounded. He believed they were going to be okay. A summer at her farm did not sound so bad.

Thomas's recovery would prove to be slow and both Pea and Mary would visit him over the next few weeks. He was finally at peace with Shawnette's loss. No more women would die the way she had. His name was cleared and he would be able to leave their apartment and move forward with his life.

He did not believe he would love another woman again. Shawnette's place could not be taken. But that was ok. He had lived a lifetime in the two years he had loved Shawnette. And he could live with that.

Trey found Pea sitting alone in the waiting room when he arrived at the hospital after finally being allowed to leave the farm house by the police. She sat staring at the wall, as if she could see all the past and present there. He sat down beside her and waited. Someone in the ER had given her a set of scrubs so the police could take the bloody clothes she had had on.

"I blamed myself for so much," she said.

He leaned back in the chair, clasped his hands together and stared a the wall with her.

"Have I lost you, too?" she asked.

He was surprised by the question, but shook his head no and took her hand in his.

"I wish you had told me more. I wish I could have done more, but" he faltered for a moment and then continued.

"I said I loved you and I do. If you still need time, take it. I'll still be here. Waiting."

She smiled at him. "No more waiting. I've waited long enough."

"Do you want me to take you back to your farm?"

"No, . . . wait, yes. I need to ask you a big favor. Could we go to your farm for a while? I told Mary to take Joseph to the farm to recuperate and I'd like to go somewhere with no memories for a while," she said.

"And this is the big part - can I bring my dogs up to your farm? I miss them and I don't want to leave them."

Trey smiled and stood, taking her hand and guiding her toward the exit.

"Yes. We'll take the dogs up to the farm. And anything else you want to take there. Anything."

The bright sunshine outside almost blinded her at first, but the day felt fresh and she had left most of her tears in that room where she had left Manley.

She stopped in the parking lot for a moment and turned to Trey.

"You know he killed more than 12 women. He killed one other person. He killed Alicia. Alicia was the 13th victim," she said.

She walked to Trey's car and took a deep breath. The past was no longer present. She looked at Trey standing beside her and for the first time saw her real future.

Reneé Porter

## ABOUT THE AUTHOR

Previously an editor and writer for non-fiction books and publications as well as an award winning author of short fiction, *The 13th Victim* is Renee Porter's first novel.

Her second novel, *Bell Park*, will be published in the summer of 2011.

Reneé Porter